PALMETTO SUMMER

BY
ELIZABETH J. GALYEN

PublishAmerica
Baltimore

© 2003 by Elizabeth J. Galyen.

All rights reserved. No part of this book may be reproduced, stored in a retrieval system, or transmitted in any form or by any means without the prior written permission of the publishers, except by a reviewer who may quote brief passages in a review to be printed in a newspaper, magazine, or journal.

First printing

ISBN: 1-59286-950-5
PUBLISHED BY PUBLISHAMERICA, LLLP
www.publishamerica.com
Baltimore

Printed in the United States of America

DEDICATION

I am dedicating my first novel to
my husband Jim and our son Dan.

They are my driving force to my accomplishments
and my best critics.
Both of them are the reasons
I look forward to each and every day.

To Linda,
A great friend and
my best friend. I couldn't have done
without you.
it without you.
Love Jamie 2003

Acknowledgements

I would not have been able to complete this novel
if not for my friends that stood beside me during the writing process.

A heartfelt thanks for her editing.
Lisa Vitaniemi
She pushed me all the way to persevere.

For those who have read the manuscript:
Chris Sunkel,
Lynda Gherna
and
Jan and Bob Trembley.

Thank you. To all of you, I will forever be indebted.

Chapter One

Sitting on the beach with the waves lapping up over her feet, Samantha feels the warm, soft air on her skin and wonders if there is anywhere in the world she would rather be than right here in Palmetto, South Carolina. She tries to come down here every evening to unwind after a hard day at the paper. As the wind is blowing her shoulder length, light brown hair she is not aware of the man leaning on the wooden railing on the pier watching her.

Her thoughts turn to her little town of Palmetto, population fifteen thousand, and what everyone else does when they get home from a normal, stressful day at work. At 29, she's still single, living alone, and not in a relationship at the moment. The pain is still too fresh from her breakup with Jacob to even think of getting into another relationship any time soon.

Samantha's lived in Palmetto since birth and has no plans of ever leaving. She loves the ocean, the people and the small town. She's about five-six, one hundred twenty five pounds with light brown hair, that's cut a little less than shoulder length and wears it parted down the middle. After graduating from college she was offered the job at the *Tribune* and had no qualms about accepting the position. She would be content living in Palmetto forever. In fact, she thought that she and Jacob had a future together in Palmetto, until he recently dumped her, not giving her any reason for the breakup.

It's been a stressful week at the newspaper. The story she hopes to be assigned to for the *Carolina Tribune*, has taken everything out of her. The mysterious death of Courtney Britton has everyone in Palmetto frightened and left with too many unanswered questions.

Courtney, also 29, was walking home alone late one evening this last week, after working at the library, and was attacked from behind, strangled and stabbed to death. It will be a very long time before she'll be able to erase that scene from her mind.

Courtney always took the same route home after working at the library and never had any trouble in the past, until now.

Palmetto is your typical little southern town where everyone can leave their homes and cars unlocked with no thought of anyone bothering anything–until now. The town is in a state of panic and grief, as everyone knew Courtney and thought the world of her. Now in the evenings parents are not letting their sons or daughters go out and be themselves. The streets are shockingly quiet after dark, and Palmetto is like a ghost town.

With summer in full swing, Palmetto is usually filled with young people out enjoying the many activities of summer in a beach town. The beaches are deserted at night, no crackling fires on the sand, no loud music or sounds from the kids as they are chasing one another on the beach.

She knows in her heart, that she will do everything in her power to do the best investigative reporting on this case that she can, that is if George, her boss, will turn her loose.

Realizing it's getting late; she pulls herself up and dusts the sand off her shorts. Walking down the beach toward the pier on her way back to her little cottage, she observes this man on the pier watching her. She feels a little uneasy, knowing what has just happened to Courtney, and realizes that it is not too smart to be out here by herself. Old habits are hard to break. The man starts walking back down the pier towards her as she approaches.

There are still a lot of other people on the pier, so she's not too worried about her safety.

As she's getting closer to him, she sees that he is extremely good looking. He seems to be about six feet tall with dark brown hair, which the wind is blowing in his face. He's wearing khaki pants, a light blue polo shirt and carrying his off-white deck shoes over his right shoulder. She's feeling a little uneasy as he approaches her because he keeps staring at her.

"Hi," he says taking the last step off the pier. "Don't I know you from somewhere? I saw you sitting on the beach over there and I thought I recognized you."

"No, I'm sorry, but I don't believe you do." She's a little skeptical at this point and starts getting an eerie chill. She continues to walk as he joins in beside her.

"I don't mean to frighten you, but I'm almost sure I've seen you somewhere before."

She realizes this guy is not from the south because of his northern accent.

"You aren't from around here are you?"

"No, I'm not," he says as he extends his arm for a handshake. "Please allow me to introduce myself. My name is Tyler Worth from Pittsburgh."

Okay, she thinks as she ignores his hand out for the handshake. Big deal. That really doesn't tell her a whole lot. Not thrilled about telling him her name, she keeps walking a little further up the beach. Seeing that they are walking away from the most populated part on the beach, she becomes even more nervous.

"I'm sorry," she says looking up at him. "But I must be going."

"Can I walk you to where you are going? You know, it's not exactly safe out here now, with the killer still on the loose from the attack earlier."

"I'm sorry, but how do I know that you are not him?"

Tyler laughs at the comment and wants to explain, when all of a sudden it hits him, where he knows her from, or at least has seen her–on the news.

"Aren't you Samantha Summers from the *Carolina Tribune*?

"Yes, I am, but how do you know?"

"I've seen you on TV, Miss Summers."

"Of course," she says gesturing with her arms. " I'm sorry. But I'm just a little jumpy."

"And rightfully so," he says looking down at her.

"I hope to work on this case. I had a close connection to Courtney. All of us in Palmetto thought a lot of her. Tragedies like this aren't supposed to happen in small towns. What is the world coming to?" she asks. "It seems just like yesterday, that you could come down to the beach at night and not have to worry about anyone bothering you. Now we can't step out of our homes that we aren't looking over our shoulders. This is such a personable little town. Everyone knows everyone else and we all pitch in whenever anyone is in need. I intend to work very closely with the police and hope that they can solve this case quickly. That is, if I get the chance."

"Are there any leads on the case yet?" Tyler inquires.

"Not anything concrete," Samantha adds. "Right now they are still trying to question anyone that might have seen or heard anything that night. Palmetto isn't that large of a town, that too much can happen without someone noticing."

She realizes as they are walking up the beach, that they're getting closer to her cottage. She's wondering at this point just what it is Mr. Worth is doing here; and, too, why he is still beside her; and just what does he want with her? She remains talking with him and senses that he isn't going to go away. She's wondering how she's going to get away from him. She's feeling something a little strange, but yet she seems comfortable talking with him. In fact she's enjoying the company a little more than she should, having just met him. What is it that makes her curious? Yes, he's good-looking—okay, very good looking–but she's feeling a little uneasy. No, uneasy isn't the word. Maybe a little flutter in her stomach is a better way to describe it. Okay, Samantha, think about what you are doing. You know absolutely nothing about this man.

"Mr. Worth?" She asks. " Just what is it that you are doing down here from Pittsburgh, and why are you interested in this case?"

"Sam, please call me Tyler, won't you?" he asks.

"My name is Samantha," she says.

"Okay, Samantha, but I feel Sam is better fit for you."

"Mr. Worth," she says. "I think I should be going. It's been nice meeting you and thank you for walking with me."

She starts walking away and realizes she doesn't want him to see where she lives. As she turns around, he is just turning away but he stops and looks back at her. She gives a slight wave to him and he continues back down the beach. She moves a little slowly as to give him time to get out of sight. Then she continues to walk towards home.

Chapter Two

Home, she fell in love with this place the first time she saw it. She thought moving out on her own would be quite an adventure. The loneliness being away from her family–mom, dad and her sister, Kaitlin–was the hardest adjustment to make. She thought it was time for her to make the move.

Venturing out on her own, trying to find the place she wanted was easier than she anticipated. When she found this place she knew it was going to be her home. She wanted a little cottage on the beach with a view of the ocean. She couldn't have asked for more. She loves the open windows facing the ocean, feeling the salty breeze.

The interior of the cottage needed little or no fixing up. A little paint and new curtains made it just what she was longing for. The couple that lived here before her had recently decorated, and it was the shabby chic, tropical look she desired. Hunting for a little furniture on her own was easy. She'd always wanted white wicker and down here in the south that was easy. When she had the minor decorating changes made that suited her, it was just as she had dreamed.

She had never been afraid to stay here alone– at least not until now. She keeps asking herself if she's safe. She can't live her life running scared, but this mess with Courtney has her a little spooked..

Walking up the front walk, with the ocean's waves lapping behind her, she feels a sense of uneasiness. "Why?" she asks herself. Is it because of what's happened, or is she thinking about Tyler and what he's doing in town, and the feelings she's experiencing when she's only just met him. "Okay, Samantha," she tells herself. "Get these thoughts out of your head and move on." She has a huge pile of paperwork she should be working on, and gee, she's hungry. She hasn't had anything to eat since lunch.

She was preparing a tuna fish sandwich as the phone rings. As she's spreading the tuna on the bread, she grabs the phone on the counter. "Hello."

"Hi, Samantha. It's Lee. How's it going?" he asks. Lee is a co-worker at the *Tribune*.

"Gee, Lee. I just left the office about an hour and a half ago you must miss me already. What's up?"

"Well, I just thought I'd call and let you know, that tomorrow when you come in the office, there will be a guy here from our other bureau, that will be helping with the investigative reporting on Courtney's case."

"What?" she inquires. " I think I'm a big girl and can handle this case on my own!"

"I'm sorry, Samantha," he says. "I know you can and you also know that I don't make any decisions. George will decide who gets the case, as you well know."

"Who is this guy anyway? Gosh, Lee, can't you do anything about this?"

"Sorry, Samantha. But I can't. I'm not any higher up the ladder than you. I'll talk to you tomorrow when you get in. I just thought I'd call and give you a little heads up."

"Yeh, thanks, Lee. I'll be sure and get even with you later. You know, I don't like working with anyone. I guess I'll have to take care of this tomorrow, since it's too late to do anything about it now. But, I will be looking for you at the office in the morning."

After hanging up the phone, her curiosity gets the best of her. What in the world are they thinking? She's lived in this town all of her life, and she doesn't need anyone helping her on this case in her own town.

She still has her article to concentrate on now. She'll deal with this tomorrow.

As she's trying to finish her article, her mind wonders. Who was this Tyler she met on the beach this evening? She can't seem to get him out of her mind. It's been a while since her breakup with Jacob, but she hasn't thought of seeing anyone since. What is it about Tyler? She still wonders what he is doing in Palmetto. Will she run into him again while he's here, or was this, the one and only time she would see him?

"Okay, Samantha," she says to herself. " Keep your mind on your work."

Chapter Three

Her alarm in her head goes off, like clockwork. Why is it that she can wake up almost every morning at the same time without relying on her alarm clock? She rolls out of bed to get into the shower when it hits her what Lee told her last night on the phone. "This is going to be an interesting day, and one that I'm sure I'll want to forget." she tells herself. "Who in the world am I going to get the privilege of meeting and working with now? Get yourself ready for work and go find out. You are only going to make yourself miserable until you know."

She arrives at work a little before 7:00 am. Most of the guys are hovering over the coffee machine having their first or second cups of coffee and eating donuts. She doesn't see anyone that she doesn't recognize, so she ventures into her office.

As she's looking over the papers on her desk, Lee comes in. "Good morning, Sunshine. How's my girl this morning?"

"Good morning to you too, or is it?" she asks. "Don't try to sweet talk me this morning. I'm not in the mood."

"Where is this guy, that's suppose to be working with me?"

"Now, don't get your bowels in an uproar. You may actually like this guy."

"Don't be too sure of yourself there Lee. You know I've had to do this before, and situations like this don't usually turn out for the best."

"Well you have about one hour and then you'll know." Lee informs her.

"Gee, thanks a whole lot. I've a memo on my desk from the boss that he wants to see me ASAP when I came in this morning so I'd better go find out what it's about."

Great. Here goes nothing. She's going to meet Mr. Wonderful sooner than she expected. Grabbing her steno pad she makes her way to George's office.

"Good morning, George," she grumbles.

"Good morning to you, Samantha. Aren't we chipper this fine morning," he states.

"I read my memo, George. What is it you want to discuss with me?"

"I'm going to send you out in the field this morning, Samantha, as an investigator on the "Courtney" case."

"You what?" she exclaims. "You really mean it?"

"Absolutely! You seem to really enjoy this part of your investigative reporting and do such a great job of it, I want you to start out on the ground floor and see what good you can do. You'd known Courtney such a long time. I feel that you can be very useful. I want you to be very careful, keep your nose clean and your eyes wide-open. Don't let anyone give you a rough time."

"Oh my God, George!" She exclaims. "Are you sure? This is really great. I was only hoping to do some articles for you and a little investigating on my own. I don't know how to thank you."

"Don't thank me yet, Samantha. Knowing you, you can get yourself into trouble without trying and you could be off this case before it even gets started," George explains.

"Oh, no, I won't. Not this time, George. I want to do this for Courtney. We can catch this guy, I know we can. I won't do anything to jeopardize my position."

"Okay, Samantha." George laughs. "Get out of here before I change my mind."

As she's almost skipping towards the door of George's office, she stops herself cold. "Am I going to do this solo?"

"No, Samantha, I haven't entirely lost my mind. Your partner will be here shortly and I'll do the introductions."

"Oh shucks, I can hardly wait," she growls, as she turns to exit out George's door. "I knew it was too good to be true. You'd never trust me out there alone."

Chapter Four

About an hour later as she's typing on a report, she's interrupted by that annoying intercom. Pushing the receive button, she hears George's voice on the other end.

"Samantha, can I see you in my office pronto?"

"Sure, I'm on my way."

Great, the time has arrived. She can hardly wait to meet him or maybe it's a her.

Approaching George's office door, she's a little apprehensive. She taps on the door and George beckons her to enter.

"Hi, Samantha. Thanks for coming in."

She sees a gentleman turned toward the window as she approaches. She's thinking this is the man she's going to be so privileged to work with. Okay, Samantha, mind your manners. This may not be as bad as you think; or who knows, it might be a nightmare.

"Samantha, I would like for you to meet Mr. Tyler Worth from Pittsburgh. He will be working with you on Courtney's case. Tyler, this is Miss Samantha Summers. She is one of the best reporters we have."

She cannot believe it. Who would have thought that this would be the same man she'd met on the beach last night. He was giving her a smile that could melt any woman. She wonders what he is thinking right now? She doesn't think she wants to read his mind.

"Have you two met?" George asks. " By the looks on both your faces it appears that you have."

"I'm sorry George. "I believe Tyler, Mr. Worth, and I met last evening on the beach."

"Yes, I believe we did George," Tyler states.

"Well, good. Have a seat the two of you and we can get started. I'd like to set some ground rules for the both of you. You two know the seriousness and danger of this case. We know the killer is still out there and we want the both of you to be extremely careful in the depth of your investigating. Don't get yourselves into trouble. Let the police do their work and keep your distance. I believe the two of you can be very helpful, but use extreme caution. Samantha, I'm counting on *you* to use your knowledge of Palmetto, and, of course, your closeness to Courtney to help Tyler unravel this thing. I'm sure both of you will do your best and *please* Samantha, do try to get along."

"*Excuse me*, George! What do you mean?"

"You know exactly what I mean, Samantha. I know you are not crazy about having someone working with you, but please just this once, do as I ask. I'm putting Tyler with you for your protection as well as for his skills in helping solve this case."

"Okay, George, I'll try, but I don't have to like it."

"Samantha," Tyler says. "Please, you don't even know me. Give me a chance to prove myself and I guarantee that you will change your mind."

"I doubt that!" she exclaims. As she's getting out of her chair, Tyler takes a hold of her elbow.

"Samantha, can we go somewhere and you can fill me in on what you know about Courtney?" Tyler asks. "I'd like to get started on this as soon as possible."

"Sure Tyler, lets get started. Let's move over to my office."

"Tyler, take care of her for me. She's a handful, but I think you'll be able to handle her."

"Goodbye George," she says. "We'll keep you posted on any developments."

Okay, she asks herself? What are you going to do now, Samantha? Why didn't Tyler tell you when you met him last night what he was doing in Palmetto? Did he already know who she was and that he was working with her on the case? She keeps walking toward her office with all of these unanswered questions rumbling in her head.

"Samantha, I think we can do this you know." Tyler says.

"Do what?" she asks.

"Work together on the case. You know what I mean."

She unlocks the door to her office and they both enter. As she rounds the corner of her desk, she glances at Tyler. "Why didn't you tell me who you were last night?"

"I honestly didn't know who I would be working with until I met with George this morning. I'm sorry Sam. I would have told you, had I known. Would it have made a difference?"

"I really don't know since I wasn't sure if I was going to get the case or not. But it would have been nice for you to tell me that you were in town to work on the case and, that I would be seeing you at the office. We've all been running a little scared, as I told you, since this whole situation with Courtney, and I was just a little cautious meeting you last night."

"Do you think we can start over and try this again? I'm looking forward to working with you on the case and I'd like to start out on the right foot. I think there is a lot we can accomplish together in trying to break this case and I need your help."

"Okay, Tyler. Where would you like to start?" She knows she's stuck with him and just maybe she should give him a chance.

"We can start by forgetting about last night and moving on."

"How about starting on the case and going from there? After all, that is what you are doing here, right?"

"That's fine with me, let's get started." He sits down in the chair in front of Samantha's desk.

Chapter Five

After discussing the case, but mostly Samantha's relationship with Courtney, for the last few hours, Tyler's getting a little hungry. "Samantha, why don't we break and have a little lunch? Do you know of any good places to grab a bite so we can discuss this further over lunch?" Tyler asks.

"Sure Tyler. But do you have an eating preference? Italian, Chinese, Mexican?" she asks. "There's a nice little restaurant just a couple of blocks down the street where we can grab a burger. Does that sound all right with you?"

"Sure, Samantha. That will be fine."

As they are leaving, George comes out of his office. "Hey you two, how's it going? Is she a handful Tyler?"

"So far so good, George." Tyler says as he smiles at her and is thinking how beautiful she is.

"Well, you just let me know if she starts getting under your skin and I'll be glad to have a little talk with her."

"George, you just stay out of this. We'll be fine and you know you don't have to worry about me."

"Yeh sure, Samantha," George laughs. "That's why I said what I did."

"Goodbye George." She says as she tugs at Tyler's sleeve to go out the door.

They had a leisurely walk to the restaurant as she was showing Tyler points of interest around Palmetto. She especially pointed out to him the library where Courtney had worked.

"How long did Courtney work at the library, Samantha?" Tyler asks.

"Oh, if I recall, I believe she had worked there since getting out of high school. She left for college, but came back here every year to work during summer vacations. She'd been at the library from graduation until the time of her death. She really enjoyed her work there. I never understood why she came back to work for them once she graduated. I would have thought a girl as bright as she would have gotten a good job and moved on. I know there were a lot of people around town who wondered the same thing."

"Was she seeing anyone at the time of her death? Tyler asks.

"No, I don't believe so." She remarks. "She very rarely dated. She was such a beautiful girl, I could never understand why," she says. "I often wondered if a boyfriend was why she kept coming home for summer vacations. But I never saw her with anyone. This is a small town as you know, and I believe I would have seen them if she did, or anyone else would have for that matter. People say she just mostly kept to herself. I really liked her and we were pretty good friends in high school, but you know how it is when you graduate and go off to college. You meet new people and sometimes your high school friendships kind of disappear."

Entering the restaurant Tyler notices someone across the street staring at them, as he opens the door for Samantha.

"Samantha, is that someone you know over there?" Tyler points across the street.

"Oh," she sighs. "Yes, that's Jacob."

"Jacob." Tyler says. "You say that like there's a problem."

"He was my former boyfriend."

Nothing more is said about Jacob as they enter the restaurant, get seated, and their orders are taken. Samantha orders a chef salad and Tyler orders a hamburger, fries, slaw and a milkshake.

"I'm famished." Tyler replies. "I didn't eat breakfast this morning."

"Eat what you want. I never eat much for lunch but I try to eat a sensible dinner."

As they are waiting for their food to arrive, Samantha tries to get away from talking about Courtney, wanting to learn a little about Tyler. She knows nothing about him, other than he is from Pittsburgh and is down here working on the case.

"Tyler. What brought you down here?" she asks.

"This case," Tyler states. "I heard that they needed someone else, so I volunteered. I haven't been down in this area for quite some time and thought it would be a good opportunity to see it again and work while I'm here. I love this part of the country with the ocean and warm soft air. I don't know what it is about it, but I love the ocean."

" Yes, I do too," she says. "I wouldn't want to live anywhere else. Are you married or have any children?"

"No, I'm not married, never been married and not really involved with anyone at the present. And of course I have no children. Like you, I'm recently out of a relationship."

"That was short and to the point," she admits.

As their food arrives they continue their conversation through the meal. She was determined to learn as much about this man as she could since she was going to spend almost all of her waking hours with him for the next several weeks.

"What about your relationship with Jacob? What happened, if you don't mind me asking?" And he takes another bite of his hamburger.

"It's really a long story and I doubt very much that you really want to hear it." It wasn't something she really wanted to get into with someone she just met. Quite frankly she hadn't even discussed it too much with her parents.

"Try me. When I saw the way you looked at him when we were outside, I got the distinct impression that it isn't really over. It seems I could see some hurt in those eyes of yours."

"Very observant of you. I was really in love with Jacob. We'd gone with each other for a little over a year. I thought everything was going great. I don't really know when our relationship started to deteriorate, but he became quite distant and started backing off. He finally said he wanted to call our relationship off and I was devastated. If I'd known the reason I could probably have understood, but I didn't and still don't. He never explained it to me. I often wondered and still do, if there was someone else. He said no, but if it wasn't someone else, why would he break up with me? I thought we had a fantastic relationship."

As she's telling this to Tyler, he reaches across the table and puts his hand over hers and she feels herself shudder. What is causing this she asks herself? She hopes he doesn't notice. He'll think she has some high school crush on him or something. As they continue talking, he doesn't remove his hand. She doesn't know whether to pull it away, even though she doesn't want to, or just let him leave it there. She finds herself just doing nothing. What harm could it do? She hasn't been with anyone since Jacob and she doesn't think she will want to be for a long time. It still hurts too much and she's not over Jacob.

"Listen to me, I'm sorry," she says. "I haven't talked to anyone close to me about this, so why am I telling you, a total stranger? This isn't like me."

"I don't know. Maybe you just needed someone to talk to. No need to apologize. I've been known to be a good listener." And as he's talking he's gently rubbing his thumb over her hand.

She doesn't know if she can handle this or not.

They finished their meal, and the waiter brings out their ticket.

"Tyler, we came here to discuss the case over our lunch and we haven't talked about it at all. I'm sorry. I guess when I saw Jacob everything else was forgotten. I need to just forget about him and move on, but I just don't seem to get over the hump."

"Shall we go back to your office, Samantha?" Tyler asks as he's pulling her chair out for her.

"Tyler, why don't I show you where Courtney was killed?"

"Okay, if that's what you want to do. We do need to get back to work though don't you think? Maybe going there will give some insight and some direction to work on."

As they're leaving the restaurant and walk back down the street, they come to the stoplight. A vehicle swerves around the corner and almost knocks both Tyler and Samantha off the curb. Tyler grabs her and pulls her back before she gets hit.

"Who in the hell was that?" Tyler asks startled. "Are you okay?"

"Yes, thank you," she exclaims trying to regain her balance. "I don't know who it was, he was going so fast. I didn't recognize the SUV either. Kids these days drive like maniacs."

If it *was* a kid, Tyler says to under his breath.

"It almost seems as if he was aiming for us." Tyler says.

"I know. There wasn't anyone else close, so why did he swerve our way? Why would anyone want to hit us?"

"I don't know. I'm new in town and don't know anyone."

"I don't know why anyone would want to do me harm either."

"Well, we'd better watch it for a while," Tyler says.

They continue walking back to the office and not much more is said about what has happened. Once back at the *Tribune* Tyler says he'll drive to the sight where Courtney was killed.

"Are you sure you're okay, Samantha? You're quivering."

"Yes, I'm okay. Thanks for asking. I just can't seem to shake it. I really feel that whoever that was, was aiming for me or both of us."

"It was probably just a teenager not paying attention to what he was doing." Tyler says putting his arm around her shoulders to guide her into the building.

"Why don't you go around and get your car while I go freshen up?"

"Are you sure you want to go now?" Tyler asks.

"Yes, I'll be fine."

Walking to his car Tyler is thinking about Samantha. Boy is she a knockout he says. Tyler, forget it. You are here to do a job not get involved. Work and pleasure do not mix.

As he's pulling around the building, Samantha comes out the front door.

"It's getting a little warm this afternoon, isn't it?" she asks as she climbs in and shuts the door.

"Yes, it is. But it's not as hot as it's going to get down here later in the summer, is it?"

"No, you're right," she says. "It gets pretty unbearable sometimes, but with the ocean breezes we constantly have, it doesn't seem as hot as it is."

"If you will make a right at the next stop sign, we'll only be about a block away."

"This is quite a pretty little town, Samantha. I can see why you like it. I love the cypress hanging in the trees, and the flowers are vibrant."

"Tyler, you can pull over right here. We'll have to park and walk the rest of the way."

There is already a police car parked in front of them. Getting out of the car they cross the street and walk to the scene where Courtney was killed. A policeman and another gentleman are exploring the scene. Yellow tape is strung around the perimeter where Courtney was found.

"Good afternoon Tom." Samantha says.

"Hello, Samantha. Please tell me you aren't working on this case."

"Yes, I am and this is Mr. Tyler Worth from Pittsburgh. He will be working with me. Tyler this is Tom Chandler, our local sheriff."

"Nice to meet you, Mr. Chandler." Tyler says.

"Just call me Tom, Mr. Chandler sounds too formal."

"Samantha and Mr. Worth, this is Captain Robert Stewart. He will be leading the investigation on Courtney's case."

"Nice to meet you Captain," Tyler states as he extends his arm for a handshake.

"Likewise." Samantha says as she shakes his hand as well.

"Samantha, you aren't going to be in my face on this case are you?" Tom asks.

"Now, Tom, would I do that?"

"Samantha, let's get one thing clear here and now. I realize I can't stop you from doing your job, but you keep your distance and your nose clean okay?" Tom asks.

"Tom," she says. "All I can promise is to do my best."

"I've worked with her before, Captain Stewart, and she thinks she runs these investigations."

"Well, we'll just have to keep our eye on her then, won't we?" Captain Stewart says as he winks at her.

"Samantha, what am I getting myself into, working with you on this case?" Tyler asks. "I know George warned me, but I thought he was just ribbing you."

Tyler's thinking too. This little number is going to be a handful and I may be in for more than I bargained for. But she had better watch out because I'm beginning to think I'm going to enjoy every moment of this, in more ways than one.

"Okay, gentlemen," she says. "Fun's over. We have a case to work on here and I think it would be best if we concentrate on it, rather than on me."

"You're right, Samantha," Tom says. "But there is no harm in teasing you a little. But I mean it when I say for you to keep your nose clean. We've already had one murder and I don't want you to be the next one. I've got enough to keep me busy without having to watch your back also?"

"Point taken, Tom," she says a little embarrassed.

"Tom?" Tyler asks. "Are there any leads so far? Or have you come up with any clues?"

"No, nothing yet. Captain Stewart just came on today. We are planning to further questioning people tomorrow."

"Can we come with you tomorrow?" Samantha asks knowing full well what the answer will be.

"No, Samantha," Tom says. "I believe we want to lay some groundwork on our own first."

"Oh," she says. "You're not going to hold this story out on me are you Tom?"

" No, Samantha I won't. "But give us a little time before you start riding us for information, will you?"

"Oh, all right," she says disgusted. "Tyler let's go see what we can do on our own."

"Okay, Samantha. Nice to meet you Tom and Captain Stewart. We'll be seeing you again soon, I'm sure."

Chapter Six

Leaving Tom and Captain Stewart, Samantha takes Tyler a little further away from the scene. He can hardly believe that this is where Courtney was killed. There is nothing secluded about the area. It's not that far from the library and certainly there should have been someone that saw something out here. It's a pretty populated area as far as people go. There seem to be many people walking here to there. It must have just been a slow evening when this occurred, or perhaps he could have dumped her here, meaning he killed her elsewhere.

"Samantha, I have the feeling something is missing here. Is it usually this populated in the evenings?"

"Yes, it's usually pretty busy most of the time, especially this time of year. There are a lot of families that are down here for the summer, now that school has let out. Evenings they like to spend time in the shops and walking down to the beach and pier."

"It just doesn't make sense to me how anyone could kill someone right here without anyone noticing."

"Well Tyler, that is something you and I are going to have to find out. What do you say we do some investigating on our own and question some people?"

"Samantha, remember what Tom said. You are not to do his job for him. Our job is to report what he and Captain Stewart find."

"They don't have to know everything I, we do, do they? Besides, I know a lot of people in this town, particularly Courtney's friends. Maybe they know more than they are willing to tell them and will confide in us. It certainly won't hurt to try."

"Samantha, I can see that you have no intentions of behaving yourself where this case is concerned. Do you think for one minute I will let you get yourself or me for that matter, in trouble with the police?"

"Tyler, I don't know about you, but I am use to taking care of myself. I am in this, with or without you. I told George I didn't need anyone, but he insisted."

"I'm in, Samantha, but please don't make me wish that I had not stepped foot in this town."

"Let's get busy then. I know someone we can talk to. The library doesn't close for about an hour yet. One of Courtney's best friends works there. Maybe we can get more out of her than Tom could."

It's pretty quiet in the car on the way to the library. Samantha's watching Tyler as he's driving down the street and he has this look on his face that tells her she'd better not even ask. She wonders just what he is thinking.

He's certainly glad that Samantha can't read his mind right now. He can tell she's watching him and he sure hopes she doesn't ask what's on his mind. He'd rather not have to explain anything just now. It really concerns him how involved she seems to get in these cases. It's obvious to him, that she has no intention of keeping her distance on this one and that he's going to have to see that she doesn't get hurt.

Thankfully they reach the library quickly, since it isn't that far from the crime scene. Palmetto is such a small community that almost everything is within walking distance.

She and Tyler enter the library. She's looking for Sara as they approach the counter.

"Hi, Lacy. Have you seen Sara?" Samantha inquires.

"Hello, Samantha. Yes, I just sent her back to the storeroom to look for a book for someone. You are welcome to go back there if you'd like."

"Thanks, I think we will."

"Tyler, this will give us a little privacy, plus we will not disturb the other people in here while we're talking."

Walking into the storeroom, she spots Sara.

"Hi, Sara."

"Oh, hi. What brings you here? I haven't seen you in a while."

"Sara, I'm here to see if you might answer a few questions for me if you would."

"Oh! I bet you are here working for the paper and wanting to know about Courtney."

"Yes, Sara, I am."

"Sara, this is Tyler Worth from Pittsburgh. He is down here to help out with the case. He's going to be doing the investigative reporting with me."

"Hello, Mr. Worth," Sara says, thinking of how handsome and well built he is.

"Nice to meet you, Sara,"

he says extending his arm to shake her hand.

"Sara, is there anything at all that you can tell us about what happened to Courtney?" Samantha asks. "Weren't you working the day she got killed?"

"Yes, Samantha, I was working that day. I don't know what help I can be to you, but if there is anything at all, I'll be more than glad to help. It has been such a shock to all of us here and in the community also. Things like this just aren't supposed to happen in Palmetto. This has always been a peaceful little town."

"Sara, did Courtney have a boyfriend?"

"No, not really. None that I knew about." Sara says shaking her head no. "Like you, I never could figure out why she would have returned here after graduation with all of the other opportunities she had been offered. I often wondered if it wasn't because of a guy, but I never saw her with anyone."

"Was there anyone that frequently came to see her here in the library?" Tyler questions.

"Courtney worked here so long, of course there were people that came here to see her?"

"Oh, I'm sure they did. But was there anyone that you would now suspect since this has happened."

"Anything you may think of, would really be appreciated Sara," Samantha says. "Even the most minute detail may be of help. If there is anything at all that you might think of later that could help Courtney, please contact me."

With her eyes tearing, Sara sniffles and says. "Samantha, we all thought so much of Courtney. I promise, if there is anything at all that I think of, I will most definitely contact you. I told the police everything I could think of.

"I'm sure you will Sara. We are sorry to have upset you. I know how hard this must be on you. You and Courtney were the best of friends, all of us were."

"Nice to have met you Sara." Tyler says. "Thanks so much for seeing us. If we can be of any help to you, let us know and also you contact Samantha if there is anything at all you think of."

As they're leaving the library, Tyler puts his hand on her elbow to lead her out the door.

"Samantha." Tyler says. "I think maybe she may be of help to us. I have this feeling she knows more than she is telling us."

"What makes you think that Tyler?"

"It's just that she was Courtney's best friend. If there was anything going on with Courtney she would have told someone, and who better than your best friend. I really think once Sara thinks about it, she will realize that the best thing for Courtney would be to find her killer. Right now she can't see past the fact that her best friend is gone. Given time I think she will be able to help us. I may completely miss my guess, but I don't think so."

"Maybe you are right," she says. "Let's give her a couple days and see if she contacts us. If not maybe we should see her again and dig a little deeper. She is really hurting now and needs time to mourn. We all do."

Exiting the library they climb into Tyler's car. Time has flown and she didn't realize it was this late. "Tyler, you can take me back to the office to get my car. There are a few things I'd like to pick up to take home and work on."

"Okay, Samantha, I can do that. Do you have any plans for dinner this evening? I'm all- alone in this town and don't know where or what there is to do. Do you mind showing a single guy around?"

I know I'm going to regret this. But what the hell, what harm can it do? She asks her- self?

"Okay. Of course I can show you around."

"Why don't I pick you up around seven and we'll go out to dinner? I love seafood and I'm sure there should be plenty of it here. How about you?"

"Yes, I love seafood. Seven sounds good."

"Another thing, Samantha." Tyler says. "I'll need directions to your house."

She gives him directions to her house as he drops her off at the office.

Chapter Seven

While she's driving home from the office she's recounting the day. Maybe working with Tyler isn't going to be so bad after all. She likes the way he dealt with Sara. He really seems compassionate about her feelings. She just hopes she can keep this a working relationship and not allow any other feelings to enter in. She thinks she could really fall for him she tells herself, but it is just too soon after Jacob. She doesn't need a relationship right now and she needs to keep reminding herself of this.

Looking at her watch she realizes that she doesn't have much time before Tyler is to pick her up. Where should they go eat, and better yet what is she going to wear? Turning into her driveway she sees headlights in her rearview mirror. They seem to be approaching at a speed too fast for her street. Just as her rear end is off the road and in the driveway, the vehicle just barely misses her tail end. "Damn it!" she screams. "Watch where you are going! Crazy people!"

Once in the house she turns on the lights and drops on the couch. "Twice in one day," she remarks to herself. "Just not my lucky day. Well you don't have much time so you'd better get your butt in the shower or Tyler will be here and you won't be ready."

About an hour later there is a knock at her door. "Well you can't say he's not prompt," She says to herself and glancing down at her watch sees it's seven o'clock.

Opening the door Tyler's standing there with a fresh bouquet of wild flowers. He looks very handsome in his navy slacks, white oxford shirt and a yellow sweater tied around his shoulders.

"These are for you, Sam." Tyler bows.

"They are just beautiful, Tyler, thank you. How did you know wild flowers are my favorite?"

"I didn't. "You just seemed the type so I thought I'd take a chance on them."

"And what is the occasion?"

"I just wanted to thank you for allowing me to work on the case with you. I know that you like to work alone and that I'm probably going to cramp your style."

"Well why don't we wait till the verdict is in. Maybe we can work together after all."

"Your home is beautiful, Sam. I'd love one day to live this close to the ocean. How did you find this place? It's great."

"I've lived in Palmetto all my life Tyler. I once said when I got a place of my own, that if at all possible, I wanted it to be as close to the ocean as I could. I was very lucky to have found this place and to have been able to obtain it. And it was in very good shape when I purchased it. I just needed to add a few of my own touches to it before I moved in."

"Would you like to see the view from outback?"

"Great, Sam. I would love too." Tyler says letting her lead him out to the back.

"Oh my God, Sam! The view is just fantastic. If I lived here I would never want to leave. You are very lucky to have such a nice house and to be this close to the ocean."

"I know and I don't ever plan on moving." Property on the ocean is so expensive I couldn't believe the deal I got on this place. Of course now days it's who you know not what. And I happen to be in the right place at the right time.

"Sam, have you decided where you want to go eat?"

"Yes, I have. There's a nice restaurant about a mile down the road that has great seafood. They also have a patio outside where we can sit, that is out over the ocean. How does that sound?"

"Okay with me. It's a nice evening and I think outside would be fantastic."

Arriving at the restaurant, they are seated outside as they requested. The view is just as beautiful as she remembers. From where they're seated they should be able to see the sunset a little later on. It's been a while since she's been here. In fact she believes the last time she was with Jacob.

"What seafood do you recommend, Sam?" Tyler asks.

"My favorite here is the butterfly shrimp or lobster."

The waitress comes to take their order and they both order the lobster. "Great choice." The waitress states. "Would you like a bottle of wine to go with your entrees?"

"Yes, we would." Tyler says. "Sam, what kind do you prefer?"

"A chardonney would be fine."

"Okay, chardonney it will be, please."

"What do you usually do on summer evenings for entertainment, Sam?"

"Not much really. Usually when I get off work I like to take a walk from my house down to the pier, just to unwind. Or I also like to just sit out on my porch and watch people and read a book. I'm not much into the nightlife anymore, so I pretty much keep to myself. I'm usually so busy with the public during the day while I'm on the job that I don't like to mingle with people during the evening. Evenings are sort of my down time. I hope that doesn't sound selfish. I don't mean for it to."

"No, not at all. I actually can relate to that very much. I'm a little that way myself. I rarely get time alone either, and when I do, I definitely take advantage of it."

"How about your parents. Where do they live?" Tyler asks.

"They live a little further inland. My father loves the ocean as I do, but my mother doesn't like to be so close. She loves the water, but is skeptical about hurricane season. She says she couldn't take it, knowing that everything we own could be taken away by a single storm. My father has his own boat business, so that brings him out here every day. Mom isn't employed, so she stays home and takes care of things. They do have a sailboat though and mom does like to go out on it. Maybe sometime when things calm down a bit or we have some free time, I can have my father take us out."

"That would be great." Tyler says. "I've only been out sailing a couple times."

"Well we'll just have to remedy that won't we?"

Samantha knows she needs to tell him what almost happened on the way home, and now might be a good time to bring it up.

"Tyler, I want to tell you what happened to me on the way home this evening after I left you. As I was pulling into my driveway I almost got hit again. Someone was coming so fast they almost clipped my rear end. Twice in one day, can you believe it?"

"Sam, why didn't you tell me this sooner?" Tyler questions. "Once I can understand, but twice in the same day. We are going to have to be careful. I think there is someone out there that doesn't like you or doesn't want you working on Courtney's case."

"Why?" she asks. "We haven't even gotten a good start yet. Why would they be after me?"

"I don't know. But you had better be extra careful."

Tyler thinking too , wonders if maybe there is more to this than Samantha is letting on. If she doesn't have anything to do with this, then why is someone after her? It could be just a coincidence, so I don't want to say much right now. I'll just have to keep my eyes and ears open and stay especially close to her. She may be innocent to the whole thing and not have a clue why someone is after her. But I don't like it.

The waitress brings the wine and Tyler makes a toast.

"To the best investigative reporting team in Palmetto!"

"Awful sure of yourself there aren't you Tyler?"

"Let's just say optimistic."

After wiping his lips with the napkin, Tyler says to Samantha. "Great choice, Sam! The lobster was perfect.

"I liked it too and I'm glad you liked it. I'm stuffed. I couldn't eat another bite if I wanted to."

"Me neither."

As Tyler looks over her shoulder he sees the sun is starting to go down.

"Sam, it looks like it's going to be a great evening for the sunset."

"I have an idea Tyler. "Why don't we go back to my place and watch it from the porch?"

"Okay, fine." He says. "But do we have time to make it back to your place before it sets?"

"Sure, that is if we leave now."

The waitress brings their ticket. Tyler pays her and explains that they are in a little hurry to see the sunset. "We have such beautiful sunsets in the summer." The waitress says. "Thanks and enjoy the rest of your evening."

"I'm sure we will." Tyler says as they're readying to leave the restaurant. "The dinner was great. Thank you for everything."

Once back at her cottage. Samantha puts on a pot of coffee. As she goes out on the front Porch, Tyler is setting in the swing.

"Oh, it's going to be a beautiful sunset this evening Tyler." She sits in the swing next to him. Once she's seated, she's asking herself if she shouldn't have sat in the chair instead. She's so use to sitting in the swing she didn't even think that this might be a little too close.

"The sunset is absolutely beautiful, Sam!" Tyler exclaims as he puts his arm around her and gives her shoulders a little squeeze. "No wonder you love it here. You have the ocean during the day and these beautiful sunsets at night. What more could a person want?"

"Before I moved this close to the ocean, I often wondered what it would be like when it stormed. I was afraid it would be eerie at night and I wouldn't like it, but it really isn't so bad. It took some getting use to, but it doesn't even bother me now."

"Would you like some coffee, Tyler?"

"No, thank you, Samantha. I'm doing just fine. In fact I'm so full I don't need another thing."

"Yeh, me too. I'm stuffed."

"Would you like to take a walk on the beach, Sam? It's still early and maybe we can walk off a little of what we ate?"

"Okay, just let me grab my sweater and I'll be right back."

"No need for that, you can wear mine. I don't need it."

Tyler puts it around her shoulders as they're walking off of the porch.

Before they know it they've reached the pier and decide to walk to the end. There is a full moon so they can easily see where they are walking. Except for a few late fishermen, the pier seems deserted.

"Catching anything?" Tyler asks one of the fishermen.

"Nope." The one explains. "I'm not having any luck at all. They don't seem to want to bite and I think I'll call it a night." And he starts reeling his line in.

They can hear the waves lapping on the walls of the pier. It's a very peaceful night. She's thinking what a nice evening this has been and how she's enjoyed Tyler's company.

Reaching the end of the pier they are looking out over the ocean and they see a big fish jump.

"I guess the fisherman was just in the wrong spot at the wrong time," she says laughingly, looking up at Tyler.

"You must be right." He says laughing back. "That would be my luck too."

Standing at the pier a little longer neither one of them is saying much. It is almost like nothing has to be said. She can feel it and is wondering if he is thinking the same thing. "Sam?" Tyler asks. She turns to look at him and can tell by the look in his eyes what she is hoping will happen next. It happens so fast she doesn't have time to react. He kisses her and she doesn't pull away. It's a soft kiss, not too little and not too much. Just enough of a kiss that she doesn't want him to pull away. "Oh my God what is happening?" She asks her- self. Just as she's wondering this, he pulls away. He is still so close though that she feels his breath on her face.

"Sam. Do you mind?" He whispers as he takes his index finger and removes a strand of hair off of her forehead and replaces it behind her ear. "I couldn't help myself. I've wanted to do that since I met you. I tried to tell myself that I had to keep this strictly on a working connection, but I can see that isn't going to happen."

"Tyler," she says as she's putting her fingers on his lips to hush him. "I don't know what I'm doing either, but it feels right."

She no sooner gets the words out of her mouth and he's kissing her again. This time he takes her chin in his hand and pulls her face to his. As their lips meet he looks into her eyes. She immediately shuts them and doesn't open them again for what seems like quite a while.

She pulls away—wondering if she's a fool or not and tells him she thinks they need to be going.

"Okay, Sam." Tyler says putting his arm around her waist and giving her a squeeze. "Let's go."

Removing his arm from around her waist, he takes her hand and leads her back down the pier. As they're heading back up the beach towards her house she takes her sandals off to feel the sand between her toes. She's always loved walking barefoot on the beach. Seeing this, Tyler does the same. The water feels good around her ankles and having Tyler next to her even feels better. Knowing her feelings are getting a little too serious too fast, she feels the need to slow things down a little before they get out of hand. As they're about to reach her house she kicks some salt water up on Tyler's backside.

"You little tease, you!" Tyler says as he pulls his right foot back. "You've ask for it now!"

He kicks water back on her and she takes off running towards the porch. She's laughing so hard she can hardly run. Reaching the porch she grabs a hold of the white round column on the porch railing to stop herself before she crashes into the door. He catches up to her at the same time and pulls her away from the column.

"You are an ornery little thing aren't you? What am I going to do with you?"

Just as he says this he pulls her against his chest and kisses her again. This time he lets her know he means business. This kiss is one she won't forget for a long time.

"I've got to be going, Sam." He says pulling away from her with fire in his eyes. "If I don't go now, I won't be responsible for my actions."

"I've had a great evening Tyler. Thank you," she says a little short of breath. She'd like to say more, but chooses not to. The right words just won't come out.

"I've had a wonderful time too, Sam." He says as he pulls her close for one last kiss. "I'll see you tomorrow at the paper."

Once back into the house she can hardly believe the evening they just shared. Since her breakup with Jacob, she thought nothing would feel this way again. How wrong she was. She knows she doesn't want to get hurt again, so she'll just have to watch what direction this is going and be very careful not to leave herself so vulnerable.

She has to remember that she just met him and is sure there is a lot about him she doesn't know and maybe wouldn't want to know. How could she have fallen so quickly when they've just met? She wonders if he thinks she's just easy or on the rebound? She definitely shouldn't have let things go this far this fast. She'll just have to step back and slow things down a little. "God, Samantha, how do you plan on doing that?" She asks herself out loud.

As she's reflecting on how things transpired this evening, she must say she actually enjoyed herself very much, maybe too much. It's just sort of how things fell into place. Everything just seemed to happen. It's not like he could have planned anything, he didn't have time. She wonders what he is thinking about now.

She no sooner finishes this thought and the phone rings as she's changing into her t-shirt and shorts.

"Sam?" Tyler asks. "I'm sorry to bother you but I just had to call. Driving back to my hotel I couldn't help but think of what happened this evening. I don't want you to think that I was too pushy. I don't normally move that fast on first dates. I can't believe what just happened, but I can honestly say I don't regret it either."

"No need to apologize Tyler. In fact, I was just thinking the same thing before you called. I don't want you to think that I'm usually that easy on my first dates. I don't think either of has an answer, so maybe we'd just better leave it at that."

"*Absolutely not!*" He exclaims. "I didn't say I didn't enjoy it, I just can't explain it happening so fast. The one thing I can say, is that I don't want to go back and undo it."

"Me neither. Why don't we take it for what it was and not rationalize? It happened for a reason and we both wanted it too. Maybe we just need to slow down and take this one step at a time. If it's to go any further from here, we'll just have to wait and see."

"Seems fair enough to me." Tyler exclaims. "Good night, Sam, and I'll see you tomorrow."

"Thanks for calling Tyler. And thank you again for a wonderful evening."

"Oh my God," she says to herself after hanging up the phone. "What kind of a team are we going to be?"

Still wound up, she fixes a glass of sweet tea and decides to spend a little time out on the back porch till she's unwound enough to go to sleep. It's getting late and she has a big day ahead tomorrow, so she knows she needs to get some sleep—but who could sleep now? Reflecting back on the day of going to the crime scene, talking to Tom and the Captain and meeting with Sara, she wonders what direction to pursue tomorrow. There are a few more people she and Tyler can interview and just maybe someone saw something. Also maybe Sara will take time to rethink that tragic day and remember something or someone unusual in the library. Tyler may have been right when he said that she knows more than she's telling them. She needs to think of all the people Courtney knew that she knows also, and maybe they need to meet with her parents. Her parents, of all people, should know who her friends were and with whom she spent most of her time. They all know she kept pretty much to herself, but she had to know someone, otherwise she wouldn't be dead now.

Chapter Eight

"Shit! Why didn't my alarm clock go off?" She asks herself. "I never do this," she says as she leans over and checks the time on the clock again. It's already 7:30 and she's to be at the office by 8:00.

She throws the covers off, flies out of bed and heads for the shower. Thank God she set the coffee pot before she went to bed last night. At least she can grab a cup on the way.

Just as she steps into the shower the phone rings. "Oh, no," she tells herself. "Not now!"

"Good morning, Sam." The voice says on the other end of the line.

"What do you want?" She shouts knowing full well it's Tyler.

"Cheerful this morning aren't we?"

"Oh, I'm sorry. I just woke up. I thought I set my alarm clock last night, but apparently I did something wrong. What's up?"

"I just wondered if I could take you out for breakfast this morning?"

"No, thank you. I'm already going to be late and I'm sure George isn't going to be too happy with me. How about a rain check?"

"Of course, Sam. I'll let you go and see you at the office later this morning. And I'm sorry, I won't delay you any longer, bye."

"Thanks Tyler, bye," she says as she hangs up the phone and gets back into the shower. "Way to go Samantha, he must think you are a real bitch. And to think he was going to take you out for breakfast. I don't get these offers very often and I just screwed that one up big time," she mumbles as she grabs the soap from the soapdish.

As she's practically running into the office she sees George looking at the big black and white clock on the wall. You might know the one morning she's late he's probably been looking for her.

"Why good morning, Samantha. We having a little trouble getting started this morning are we?" He just loves to tease her. She is always so conscious about her job, he never has cause to tease her about it, but he usually finds some other reason.

"I'm sorry George. My alarm clock didn't go off this morning." She sees him snicker as she rushes into her office.

"When you get settled, I'd like to see you in my office Samantha."

"I'll be right there. Just give me a couple minutes to get my office opened up."

She gets her door opened, grabs a can of pop out of her little fridge that she keeps in her office and heads for George's office. She's wondering what he has on his mind as she opens the can and takes a drink.

"How'd it go yesterday?" He asks.

"What do you mean how did it go yesterday?

"I mean how did you and Mr. Worth get along? I know that you weren't too crazy about having someone working with you on this case."

"Well George we did okay for the first day." She's not going to tell him everything, as he would not be a very happy camper if he knew just how well they'd hit it off. What he doesn't know won't hurt him. She's sure he would tell her that a relationship would hinder their working together on the case and worry that they would be jeopardizing their safety.

"Did you by any chance get any leads?"

"No, not yet. I took Tyler, I mean Mr. Worth, to the crime scene and we had a look around there. Tom and Captain Robert Stewart were there when we arrived. Tom gave me my orders as usual. I expected that though. Then we went over to the library to talk to Sara. I thought maybe if we questioned her, we might just get lucky. She's still pretty emotional and couldn't help us. Tyler, I mean Mr. Worth, seems to think that she probably knows more than she's telling us, but is afraid. We're going to give her a few days and then approach her again. He feels that she may know more than she thinks she knows and doesn't realize what little details can help. She's a pretty complex girl."

"Did you get a chance to talk to anyone else?"

"No, we didn't, we ran out of time."

"I just thought maybe the two of you came up with enough that we could print a story that might scare the murderer a little or at least keep him on his or her toes."

"I'm afraid not George. We're going today to talk to Courtney's parents. I just hope it's not too soon. I've known them for a long time and hope that will make them feel a little more comfortable talking with me."

"Well, you two take it easy on them. I'm sure they will want to help, but it's still awfully soon for them, but I realize we can't wait too long. I know Tom and Captain Stewart have already been there so don't push it. You may need to give them a day or two."

"Where is Tyler, Mr. Worth, anyway?"

"Samantha, why do you keep trying to call him by his first name? Remember you are suppose to be on a professional basis here," George warns her.

"I don't know George, I'm sorry. From now on it will be Mr. Worth."

"He called a little while ago and said he'd be here in about an hour."

"Great. I can catch up on some of my paperwork while I'm waiting."

She looks up at the clock and it's already 9:30. Where can he be? If they are going to get anything done this morning he had better be showing up soon. She'd like to have time to question Courtney's parents and possibly talk to a couple of her other girlfriends, plus her boss.

She's almost completed her paperwork when she sees him. He's coming out of George's office headed for hers. She must have missed him when he came in.

"Good morning Samantha. I see you finally made it." He jests with a smile on his face.

"Okay, not you too. I'm late one morning and everyone is all over me."

"And where were you I might ask?"

"I knew you were going to be running a little late so I called George and told him I'd be in a little later. I had a few things I needed to check on back at my office in Pittsburgh and felt that this would give me an opportunity to do so without using up any of our time here on the case."

"Fine. Then let's get going shall we? I'd like to question Courtney's parents.

I feel that they will talk to me, but George thinks it may be too soon since they've been drilled by Tom and Captain Stewart."

"I'm ready." Tyler says. "Let's get going."

"You two be careful." George says. "Stay with her Tyler and keep her out of trouble."

"I will George. I know what to do with her if she doesn't," he says as he winks at her from an angle that George cannot see.

"If you get anything at all you think we can report, call me and I'll see what I can get printed in today's paper."

"Okay George," she says. "But don't hold your breath."

Tyler and Samantha arrive at Courtney's parents' home. It's been quite a while since she's talked with Charles or Nancy Britton.

She knocks on the door and they are greeted by Nancy. She can tell by the dark circles under her eyes that she isn't doing well. Her mother wouldn't be either she's sure, if this would have happened to her.

"Good morning Mrs. Britton. I'm Samantha Summers from the *Carolina Tribune*. I don't know if you remember me, but I was a friend of Courtney's."

"Of course, Samantha, I remember you. Won't you come in?"

"Thank you Mrs. Britton. This is Mr. Tyler Worth. He is working with me on Courtney's case."

"Hello, Mr. Worth." She says. "Nice to meet you."

"Charles!" Mrs. Britton shouts as she turns her head toward the staircase. "We have some visitors. Would you mind coming down for a few minutes please?"

Charles comes down the stairs and Samantha must say she can't believe how he looks. This man looks totally devastated. She glances at Tyler as he's coming down and she can tell by the look on Tyler's face that this isn't going to be easy. He was unshaven, his hair needed combed and he had dark circles under his eyes. But what could they expect when he'd just lost his daughter and she was murdered no less.

"Charles, this is, Samantha Summers, from the *Carolina Tribune* and she was also a friend of Courtney's."

"Yes, I remember." Mr. Britton says. "How are you, Samantha? It's been a while since we've seen you."

"Fine, thank you Mr. Britton. I'm so sorry about Courtney. I was at her funeral, but I don't believe either of you saw me. It was a very nice service."

"Thank you, Samantha." Says Mrs. Britton. "It's been very hard on us."

"Mr. Britton, this is Mr. Tyler Worth. He is down here from Pittsburgh to work on Courtney's case with me. If you don't mind we would like to ask you a few questions."

"We know that you have already been questioned." She says.

"And at quite length." Mr. Britton says running his hand over his face. "But I don't mind. We'll try to be of help to you. We just want Courtney's killer found and brought to justice."

She sees the tears welling up in his eyes. How could anyone get through this?

"Was Courtney seeing anyone at the time?" Samantha asks.

"No." Mrs. Britton replies. "Not that we knew of. Courtney pretty much kept to herself. At one time I thought maybe she was seeing someone, but she never told me and I never was sure I was right. She started taking more interest in herself and how she looked. I was hoping that this meant she did have a boyfriend, but she said no when I questioned her about it. I wasn't quite convinced at the time, but I didn't have anything solid to base my assumptions on, so I never questioned her again."

"What about you Mr. Britton." Tyler inquires. "Did you have any reason to believe she had been seeing anyone?"

"Well about the time Nancy said she thought that Courtney was seeing someone I sort of had my suspicions also. Never anything concrete though. I also noticed that she was showing a little more interest in her appearance. But Courtney would never tell me if she was. Her life was very personal and she wouldn't share it with either one of us. We don't know why though. We were both very close to her. But she kept her personal life very private, like I said."

"Where did she attend college?" Tyler questions.

"She attended the university." Mrs. Britton stated. "Did she ever mention anyone in particular while she was there? Meaning any male or female friends?"

"No, she never really had many while she was there, only her roommate." Mrs. Britton says. "They always seemed to get along well. Their personalities were pretty close. Her roommate never use to socialize much with others either. Most of the time it would just be the two of them. Courtney would bring her home with her from time to time and we got to know her pretty well. But as far as campus activities go, Courtney never got into that."

"What was her roommate's name and where was she from?" Tyler asked. "We may wish to question her if we feel it's necessary."

"Her name is Amanda Jeffers and she was from the Myrtle Beach area," said Mrs. Britton.

"Was there anyone that you can recall that Courtney disliked for one reason or another? Samantha asks. "Like anyone who would frequent the library, become a nuisance or cause Courtney trouble and would bring home the stories after a day at the library?"

"Samantha." Mrs. Britton says. "Courtney dearly loved her job at the library. That was her life. We often wondered why she came back here after graduating from college. She had so much potential. But all she wanted to do was be here and work at the library. If there was someone causing problems or giving Courtney a rough time she never said. She would just take it all in stride. That library was her life. I think her dream was to one day be able to run it on her own. She practically did anyway."

"We sure haven't been of much help have we?" Mr. Britton states.

"That's okay." Tyler says. "We'll just have to keep digging. Samantha is determined on this one and I'm sure she will not leave a single stone unturned."

Mrs. Britton starts to cry now and Samantha can see that they've stayed long enough.

"Mr. and Mrs. Britton, we would like to thank you for your time. We know that this has been extremely hard on the both of you, but if you can think of even the smallest detail would you please call?" She asks as she reaches into her purse and hands her one of her business cards.

"Yes, thank you for your time Mr. and Mrs. Britton." Tyler says. "It's been a pleasure meeting both of you. I am very sorry about your daughter and I can assure you that Samantha, and I will do all that we can to help find Courtney's murderer."

"If you find out anything at all, would you contact us, Samantha?" Mr. Britton asks. "At this point any news at all would be a comfort. We both hope this isn't a long drawn out affair and Courtney's killer is found quickly. I don't think either one of us can take much more."

"We will do the best we can. Of course we are just investigative reporters and we have to leave the job to the police and the detectives, but that doesn't mean we can't help as long as we don't step on their toes or get in the way."

"Thanks again." Samantha says as they are walking out the door. "Just remember to call if you think of anything."

Tyler shakes Mr. Britton's hand as he's opening the door to leave. Walking back to the car he's thinking how tragic it is that the Britton's have to go through this.

"Sam, are you okay?" Tyler asks.

"Yes, I'm okay. I just can't help but feel sorry for them. That was their only child. I know Courtney was a little different, but she was very likeable and I just cannot think of who would want to kill her and why."

"Sam, let's drive by the crime scene again. I'd like to take another look around. I don't remember what businesses I saw around there close. Maybe we need to question the merchants there and the places where she frequented. We may get lucky."

"Okay by me."

"Something's been on my mind, Sam." Tyler says. "And I want you to hear me out before you say anything."

"Okay, what is it?"

"Promise me you won't say anything until I'm through."

"I promise!" She shouts. "You obviously don't think I will, do you?"

"No, I don't."

"Well I'll prove to you I can keep my mouth shut," she laughs.

"This will be a first I'm sure," Tyler says remembering what George told him about Samantha.

"Now I'm serious okay?"

"Okay." She says as she tries to keep a straight face seeing he really is serious.

"I've been wondering if Courtney didn't have a boyfriend. I've seen her type before. You know the old saying. It's the quiet ones you have to watch. From what everyone is saying, the mental picture I have of her is someone introverted, dressed down as to not draw attention, and kept to herself. I'm also wondering if maybe we shouldn't visit the university and question some of her professors and see just what their observations of Courtney were. She may have been a completely different person there than she was here. Maybe there were two sides to her."

"Oh my god Tyler!" She exclaimed. "Do you think you could really be right? I can hardly believe it because I've known her so long, but I suppose she could have gone off to college and become a completely different person. I wouldn't have thought of that. It might be worth a try. What have we got to lose?"

"The way I see it, nothing." Tyler says. "The Fourth of July is coming up so I can't see us going until after then. No one would be at the university anyway. Remember it's summer vacation, but some of her professors may be teaching summer school. Maybe we'll luck out. And if they aren't there I'm reasonably sure the personnel office would help us out with addresses and phone numbers. That is if they aren't on vacation out of town."

"That's just a chance I feel is worth taking," she says. "You know you may be way off base here Tyler. In fact I can't see her being two personalities, but who am I to say. At this point I'll try anything. My god Tyler, if you are right, what will this do to her parents? This would definitely be a story. I think we should take this scenario to George before we do anything. What do you think?"

"I agree, Sam. Let's keep our noses clean here. Not a word of this can get out until we've checked it out. Like you said, we may be way off base here, but I have this hunch. We definitely want George's approval on this. Why don't we go there first, instead of back to the crime scene and throw this past him?"

"Okay Tyler," as she shakes her head. "George isn't going to believe this one."

"Probably not, Sam, but I don't think he will turn us down on the idea either, once he's heard our point. Well we'll just have to find out won't we?" Tyler exclaims.

Driving back to the office neither one of them says much. Samantha thinks their heads are spinning in all directions. She knows hers is. Where did Tyler ever come up with this idea, she doesn't know, but guesses it's worth a try. He was whom George wanted to work with her on the case and there were reasons for it. He must have an insight on such things and this must be why. This would have never been even close to anything she would have predicted about Courtney and he may be way off base, but who knows.

Mr. and Mrs. Britton deserve answers and want them no matter what the consequences. It would really be a shock to them. If she did have a boyfriend, who would it be? She can't even imagine, but there is no use speculating yet.

They arrive back at the *Tribune* and George happens to be in his office. Usually by now he's out to lunch, but fortunately they've caught him before he left. By the time they're through with him he'll probably wish he were out to lunch. They are definitely going to make his day.

Knocking on his door Samantha hears him say for them to come on in.

"George," Samantha says. "Mr. Worth has something he would like to discuss with you concerning Courtney. Would you have a few minutes to hear him out?"

"Of course, I think I can take a few minutes. I have a luncheon date at the club but not until 12:30."

"George, we've just come from talking with Courtney's parents." Tyler says.

"So you did get to talk with them then?" He asks.

"Yes, as a matter of fact, we did," she says. "I'm really glad we did too. I don't think anyone will be able to talk to them at great length now though. They, of course, are devastated. They weren't much help though. They couldn't shed any new light on anything we didn't already know about Courtney."

"George, I have an idea I'd like for Samantha and I to check out." Tyler says. "From what I'm hearing about Courtney she was quiet, kept to herself and had few friends. Like I was telling Samantha, I have a hunch. I think we have a case here of a split personality. I was wondering if maybe Courtney went away to college and it completely changed her. Maybe she met someone and wasn't the same person at school as she was at home. "

"You may have a point there, Tyler." George says. "I must admit it's a little far fetched but it might be something to track. My god I feel sorry for her parents if this is true. It would be awfully hard for them to swallow. That is not the theory he had on her but it could be true. Just what is your plan? "

"I told Samantha, I think we need to go to the university and look up some of Courtney's professors. I'd like to wait until after the 4th though because the school will be closed and most of the professors will be on summer vacation anyway. We may just get lucky and maybe one or more of her professors might be teaching summer school. If not, we can check with the personnel office to see if they would give us names and phone numbers of a couple. I'd like to keep this under wraps at this point though George. I wouldn't want Tom or Captain Stewart to get wind of this before we had our chance to get our story."

"No chance!" George exclaims. "We want Courtney's killer caught, yes; but we also want the story. We will keep this just between the three of us until the time comes to involve the police. If this doesn't go anywhere then no one has to know a thing. I wouldn't want information like this to get out if there's not a chance that it's true. Courtney was a good person and I wouldn't want her reputation to be blemished with false accusations."

"We feel the same way George," Samantha says. "It really seems far fetched to me, but I think it warrants being checked out. It's hard telling what we might find at the university."

"So what are you going to do in the meantime?" George asks.

"Mr. Worth would like to talk to some of the merchants that own the businesses around where Courtney was murdered. Maybe they know of someone hanging around or near the library that aren't regulars or may have seen someone with Courtney."

"Fine," George says. "But I hope you have some news for us soon. We have a paper to publish here and you are suppose to be supplying us with news."

"We are doing our best George," she says. "Just don't give up on us yet okay?"

"Okay," George says. "Now the two of you get out of here. I have a lunch date of which I'm going to be late. Now scoot."

Tyler and Samantha used the rest of the week to question more people. They talked with merchants, friends and more of Courtney's family members. There hasn't been much light shed on the case. Most of them said that they rarely saw her. She kept pretty much to herself and wasn't in their stores that often or they didn't notice her comings and goings from the library. She just kind of blended in. One or two of the merchants thought they might have seen her with a guy, but couldn't swear to it, or if it was even Courtney. No one really paid much attention–until she was murdered. In a small town like Palmetto they said these things just didn't happen and everyone's guard was down. Of course with the tourist season in full swing, there are a lot of strangers in town. No one seems to notice, until something specific happens.

They did manage to question Sara again. Tyler questioned her this time and used another approach concerning the inclinations they were pursuing now. But Sara didn't suspect anything, but she had no answers either. As far as she knew, or was telling them Courtney was the quiet girl everyone thought she was. However, Tyler wasn't buying it. He said if anyone knew the true Courtney, Sara would. He still thinks Sara is holding back on them. They've decided not to pressure her anymore until they've had time to visit the university and see if Tyler's theory plays out first. If they can get something concrete they'll come back and approach Sara again. This time if they can fill in the blanks maybe she will be a little more willing to talk to them. If however, Tyler misses his guess, he doesn't want any of this to reflect on Courtney.

Chapter Nine

Tyler and Samantha had a tiring week. It's the 4th of July weekend coming up. She hasn't made any plans this year. Her parents are out of town on vacation. They've gone to visit her aunt in Florida, so she won't be spending the 4th with them and she's wondering how she will entertain herself over the weekend. She wonders what Tyler will be doing? Will he go home in Pittsburgh or is he planning to stay here?

The two of them have maintained their distance over the last couple of weeks. Most of their time has been spent questioning so many people, that they haven't spent much time together outside of work. Since they decided to cool it due to their working relationship, she doesn't know where she stands. She wonders if out of courtesy she should ask him what his plans are. She wouldn't want him to be alone for the holiday weekend. There is a lot going on in Palmetto over the 4th.

She decides to give him a call in his office. It's almost four o'clock and he won't be in much longer.

"Hello. This is Mr. Worth's office, may I help you?"

"Hi!" She says. "I know it's getting late and you are probably on your way out."

"Yes, I am, Sam, but I have a few minutes. What's on your mind?"

"Well, I was just thinking about the weekend coming up and wondered if you've made any plans? I didn't know if you were planning to go back to Pittsburgh for the weekend or staying here."

"No, Sam, I'm not planning to go back to Pittsburgh. I thought I'd stay here. I've heard they have quite a celebration right here in Palmetto."

"Yes, they do. I usually spend the weekend with my parents, but they are away visiting my aunt in Florida. Would you like to spend the weekend with me? I can show you our southern hospitality."

"That would be nice. I'd like that. We haven't had much time together recently, other than working on the case and I think both of us are due a nice weekend. What do you have in mind?"

"I'll tell you what Tyler, be at my house at 9:00 tomorrow morning. Dress casually and bring your bathing suit." That was quick talking on her part, however she hadn't yet planned anything. But in Palmetto on the weekend you definitely could use a bathing suit.

"Yes, Mam!" Tyler exclaims. "Is there anything else I need to bring?"

"No, I'll take care of everything from here."

"I'll see you at nine sharp then, Sam, thank you."

"Don't thank me until you see what I have planned."

"No, I'm thanking you for thinking of me. You could leave me all alone on the 4th, then what would I do? All alone in a town where I know virtually no one."

Hanging up she realizes she doesn't have much time to prepare for the weekend. She's just told Tyler to be at her place by nine o'clock in the morning. She's really going to have to shake a leg now, in order to be ready by morning.

Thinking to herself, she makes mental notes of what to plan for the weekend. She's been thinking about this a little and since her parents are out of town, it sure would be nice to take the sailboat out. She's wondering if the two of them can handle it. Sure they can. She knows enough about it that she can with Tyler's help. She'll fix a picnic lunch to take out with them. The fireworks are always better to watch from the boat out over the water.

Once home, she changes her clothes and gets comfortable for the evening. She's already stopped and gotten groceries, picked up some wine at the local liquor store and made a stop at the local bakery.

She keeps herself busy preparing hoagies with the bread she picked up at the bakery. She figures they'll want something they can grab to eat and go. She won't want to take time to prepare anything on the boat. She'll also make potato salad and she'll throw in a bag of chips. The brownies she picked up at the bakery should finish off the meal nicely.

After everything is completed she almost drops onto the couch. It's been a long day and she needs to get to bed early for the long weekend. She's really looking forward to spending time with Tyler and wonders what the weather is going to be this weekend. She's been so busy she hasn't even caught the news. She turns on the TV to the weather channel for the local forecast. Fortunately she sees it's going to be a beautiful weekend. No rain forecasted, or any high winds. It should be great for sailing. She's already getting excited and hopes Tyler is looking forward to it also.

She drags herself off of the couch and decides to take a shower to help her relax. Just as she's ready to step into the shower the phone rings. Grabbing a towel she reaches for the phone.

"Hi, honey, how are you?"

"Hi, Mom, I'm just fine. How's the vacation going?"

"Great! I just called to see if you've made any plans for the weekend?"

"As a matter of fact, yes, I have. Remember me telling you about Tyler, who's working with me on Courtney's case?"

"Yes, are you going to tell me that you're going to spend the weekend with him?"

"Yes, Mom, I am. I asked him if he was going home and he said no, so I thought it'd be nice to ask if he wanted to spend the weekend with me."

"*Samantha*, is there anything going on between the two of you? I have a feeling you're not telling me everything?"

"Well mom I'm not sure. I think a lot of him, but we hardly know each other. There might be something there, and if there is I'm sure this weekend will tell. We've been working so hard on the case we haven't had much time to spend together socially."

"I think that's great, Samantha. I was worried about you being alone and as usual, I'm worrying for nothing. It's nice to hear that you may be seeing someone again. I know how devastated you were over Jacob. Just be careful and make sure you know what you're getting yourself into. I'd hate to see you get hurt again."

"I know mom. I couldn't stand for that to happen again either. I'm going to be especially careful this time."

"What is he like?"

"Oh, he's tall, dark and handsome and has a great personality. I've only been out with him once, so I'm just getting to know him. Hopefully I'll be able to tell you more after this weekend mom."

"What have you got planned for the weekend?"

"I didn't tell him. I want it to be a surprise. I've just fixed everything for a picnic lunch. I thought a picnic would be fun and the weather is going to be perfect. You don't think dad would mind if we took out the sailboat do you?"

"No, honey, I think it'll be just fine. The two of you be careful though. I know you know how to sail, but do you suppose he does?"

"I don't know, I didn't ask him because I want it to be a surprise."

"Well, have a good time and I'll call you the first of the week."

"Thanks, Mom. You and dad have a good time too. I love you and will talk to you later, bye."

She hangs up the phone and jumps into the shower. The nice hot shower feels great after the long day she's had. She thinks of how nice it was for her mom to call. Her mom's been concerned about her since the breakup with Jacob. She knew she needed time to heal so she's been great about giving her space, but she also knows she cares. She just wants to spend the weekend with Tyler and have a good time. She really feels she needs to move on and put Jacob behind her. She knows it hasn't been easy, but maybe it just wasn't meant to be.

After showering, she put on her yellow and green plaid cotton shorts and yellow t-shirt and climbed into bed. In hardly any time at all she's sound asleep.

She'd set her alarm to go off at 7:30. She figured she wouldn't need much time since she prepared everything for the picnic last night. She goes to her closet to decide what she wants to wear today and finally settles for her one-piece bathing suit, a white pair of shorts, red short sleeve shirt and her navy oxford long sleeve shirt in case it gets breezy in the evening.

Once dressed she goes to the kitchen to collect everything she's taking for the picnic. She'd already dug out her picnic basket last night, so all she had to do was retrieve everything from the refrigerator and pack the basket.

She's making mental notes to make sure she has everything, hoagies, potato salad, chips, brownies and a bottle of White Zinfandel. Looks like she has everything.

Just as she'd rechecked her mental list, she heard the doorbell ring. Looking down at her watch it's nine a.m. on the nose.

"Good morning Tyler, come on in," she says as she's pulling the door open to let him enter.

"Good morning to you too, Sam," Tyler says as he steps in the door. "You look cute today in your white shorts and shirt.

"Thank you. And I might say you look mighty fine yourself."

"You're right on time." She can't believe how he looks. He's dressed in a khaki pair of shorts and navy sports shirt. He'd turn every girl's head the way he looks. But he's hers for the whole weekend."

"Did you bring your bathing suit?"

"Yes, I did. It's in the car."

"I have a picnic basket in the kitchen we'll need to get and I need to go into my bedroom for my bathing suit."

"I'll get the picnic basket and you can get your suit."

"Just where are we going, Sam?"

"It probably would be a good idea if I enlighten you on my plans wouldn't it?" She says smiling up at him.

"It just might be a good idea if you want *me* to tag along."

"I thought we'd spend the day on my dad's sailboat, if that's okay by you."

"*Oh my god Sam, that would be great*! It's going to be a perfect day for sailing. But do you think it will be okay with your father if we take it out?"

"Yes. My mother called and checked in on me last night and I asked her that very question. She said it would be fine. She's aware that I know how to sail it, but I can honestly say she hoped you'd know a little about sailing to."

"I've been on a sailboat a couple of times and sort of watched how it was done. I think between the two of us, we shouldn't have much trouble."

"Good, then let's get going."

"You lead the way and I'll follow."

They were lucky that her father had the sailboat already at the dock. He knew they wouldn't be gone that long and he always has someone looking after it anyway, so it was basically ready to go. It didn't take long for them to check it out and get everything on board. Tyler was very helpful, even though he was shocked to see just how big the sailboat was.

They spent most of the morning sailing and just enjoying the sights. There were numerous boats on the water due to the peak summer month and of course the 4th of July weekend. They really enjoyed seeing all of the different colors of sails. The sight was just beautiful. There was just enough of a breeze to keep the sailboat going and they didn't have to maneuver it all of the time.

"I think I'll change into my suit and take a swim before lunch, how's that sound?"

"That's fine. I'm not all that hungry yet anyway. I'll put my suit on also."

Tyler had changed before her obviously, and is waiting for her on deck. She feels a little self-conscious with him seeing her in her suit as she's coming up the steps from below, but she's immediately put at ease by his reaction.

"Wow, Sam! You look absolutely fantastic in that suit."

"Thank you," she says, knowing full well that her face is as red as her suit."

Tyler sees that he has embarrassed her and walks over to her and takes her hand in his. He plants a kiss on her palm and notices that this really makes her feel uneasy.

"I'm sorry, Sam. I didn't mean to embarrass you, but you looked so incredible when you came up those stairs, I just had to say something."

"That's okay. I was just a little embarrassed that's all. Shall we dive in?" She needs to do something to change the subject from herself. And she notices he looks very good in his suit also, but she wasn't about to comment or she would embarrass herself further.

They both dove into the water and swam around a little. The water felt great. Samantha came up for air and didn't see Tyler. Turning around in the water she couldn't see him anywhere. She was wondering where he could have gone, when all of a sudden she feels a hand pull on her leg. He was trying to pull her under. She kicks at him to release her leg and to no avail. One big gulp and she was under. She finally works her self loose and comes up for air. He was already above water and laughing at her as she was coughing and trying to catch her breath.

"You're going to regret doing that to me. I *will* get even." Just about that time she dives under the water and goes after him. She doesn't know what she thought she could do because he had more strength to fight her off and under she went again. This time she was really gasping when she came up. She guessed he feels sorry for her and extends his hand for her to grab a hold of and he pulls her into him.

"I'm sorry." He says laughing. "I didn't mean to drown you."

"Well you did a pretty good job of it," she says as she proceeds to splash water in his face.

He pulls her towards him again but this time he doesn't send her under. As he's trying to tread water he put his arms around her and pulls her close. She puts her arms around his neck to help keep herself afloat. He kisses her and she almost melts in his arms. She can feel his wet hands on her naked back.

"Sam, I've wanted to do that again since that night at your house," he says as he smoothes her wet hair out of her eyes. "I've had to wait too long." He says as he kisses her again. "Are you about ready to go back aboard?"

"Yes," she says, feeling his body so close to hers. .

Boosting her from behind, he helps her climb the ladder aboard first and then he climbs up after her. Her legs are shaking and are about to go out from under her. She's wondering just what affect he has on her as he comes up behind her and puts his arms around her and turns her towards him. He has retrieved a towel and proceeds to dry her off. He then wraps the towel around her and pulls her into his arms and kisses her again.

"Sam, what am I going to do with you?" He asks letting the towel drop to the deck. "You have awakened every feeling in my body, that I thought was dead."

"I know what you mean, I feel the same way," she says as she starts to shiver.

He kisses her forehead then takes her hand and leads her down below deck. Just as they reach the lower deck he takes her in his arms and kisses her again as she feels him start to release one of the straps on her shoulder. She starts to tremble.

"Are you cold or are you scared?" He asks as he looks into her eyes.

"A little scared I think," she says as she's starting to melt even though she's still shivering.

"Sam, I won't hurt you. And I don't mean that physically."

"I know. But I don't know if I'm ready for this or not."

"You tell me to stop right now, Sam, and I will," he says looking into her eyes.

"The thing is, that's what I'm afraid of most. I don't think I want you to stop. I can't believe I'm feeling this way. I barely know you."

"Then it must be right." He says and as he continues to remove the other strap over her shoulder. He's pulling her suit down over her breasts as he's looking at her. "Sam, you are beautiful," he says as he tilts his head down looking at her body.

"*Tyler*," she says as he's pulling her back up to face him. He kisses her again to silence her and is leading her toward the bed. The galley isn't that big so they are very close to it anyway and as he sits down, she ends up on his lap. He's kissing her and at the same time he's lying her down on the bed. She has her arms around his neck and he gently comes down on top of her.

Rolling over beside her he finishes removing her suit and disposes of his also. They're both exploring each other's bodies with their hands when he rolls over on top of her. As their eyes meet he kisses her and she shuts hers.

"Sam." He whispers to her. "Open your eyes. I want to look into them when I make love to you," he says as he kisses the tip of her nose.

She swears she's never felt like this before, nor has she ever been treated so gently. The look in his eyes as he's making love to her and the gentleness, in which he does, puts her into orbit.

When they are both spent, he rolls over and lies next to her. Neither one of them says anything for a few minutes. They are both just enjoying the moment.

"Sam, that was wonderful." He says as he's kissing her on the top of her head. She rolls over and rests her head on his shoulder. "Yes, Tyler, it was for me too." Nothing else needed to be said at that time, they just laid there and enjoyed each other.

She wakes up with a start. Looking over she sees Tyler still lying beside her with his arm resting on her bare stomach. She smiles remembering what has transpired and sees him smiling back over at her. "What are you smiling at?" She asks.

"You." Tyler says rubbing his thumb over her stomach.

"What do you think we should do about this?"

"Do about what?"

"Do you think we can still work together and be a good team or would you rather I pull myself off of the case? I'd do that you know, as not to jeopardize the case nor our relationship."

"*No,* I don't want you to. I think we can still work together and be a good team. I'm seeing what you can do, and I think for Courtney's sake, you should stay on. We are both adults and we can work through this. I don't know how pleased George will be when he finds out, but I'm pretty sure he can deal with it, as long as our feelings for one another don't interfere."

"It's okay with me. Besides, if I were not on the case I'd have to report back to Pittsburgh and that would be too far away from you." He says as he pulls her closer and kisses her again. Knowing full well if they didn't get up soon, they wouldn't for quite a while.

"What did you bring in that picnic basket of yours, Sam? I'm famished!" Tyler says as he's pulling his arm out from under her, while attempting to get out of bed.

She's climbing out of the bed also and he proceeds to pull her close one more time. They are both standing there totally naked, almost as one. He looks down into her eyes as he puts one of his hands on the back of her head and the other one on her buttocks and gives her the most tender kiss she believes she's ever had.

"Now get some clothes on and get that picnic basket," he says as he swats her on the butt.

After dressing, Samantha goes up on deck and spreads the white cotton blanket that she brought from home out on the deck, while Tyler stands at the front of the boat watching the other sailboats. When she has everything placed on the blanket, she asks him if he would like to open the wine.

"You've prepared quite a feast here, haven't you?"

"I know from experience that whenever our family would take the sailboat out for an afternoon, we'd all be pretty hungry after all of the sailing and swimming."

"I'm sure you have many fond memories of your times out here with your family," he says as he pops the cork and proceeds to pour the wine.

"Yes, I have. There has never a 4th of July gone by that we haven't come out here as a family, until this one.

But I guess as we get older things change. Thanks for spending this one out here with me," she says as she motions with her hand for him to take a seat on the blanket.

"You're entirely welcome, but I should be the one thanking you. Without your invitation I would have been spending it alone. How about a toast?"

"Okay, but you do the honors," she says as she lowers herself onto the blanket beside him.

"To a wonderful beginning and to an even better rest of the weekend." He toasts as their glasses clink and he leans over to seal it with a kiss.

"Now let's eat, I'm starved." She says while picking up her plate.

It had gotten later in the afternoon than they thought. They decided to sail around a little while longer until the sun started to set. Samantha showed Tyler some of the points of interest as they sailed along the coast. He was amazed at some of the homes she pointed out.

It was almost time for the fireworks to begin.

"Would you like to watch the fireworks from the shore rather than the boat?" Samantha asked.

"*Absolutely not*! I've only watched them once before on the water and there is nothing any more beautiful than watching them out here.

"Great! That's what I'd hoped you say," as she notices that most of the other boats are starting to congregate in one area from the shore to watch. They select their spot and anchor the sailboat.

"Look at all the people gathering on the shore to watch. You wouldn't think there could be that many people in Palmetto that would come out to watch fireworks."

"Oh, you'd be surprised. With all of the tourists our population skyrockets in the summer, especially now."

The first of the fireworks lit up the sky. They spread their blanket that also served as their tablecloth on the deck and sat down to watch. Tyler sat down first, then pulled Samantha down in front of him and positioned her between his legs so she could lean her back into his chest.

This feels great, thinking to herself as she unconsciously nestled a little closer into Tyler. He must have noticed this because he tightened his arms around her and gave her a kiss on the back of her neck. She's in seventh heaven. It's been a long time since a man has been this attentive to her, if ever.

The fireworks seem to go on forever. Samantha doesn't remember them ever being quite this long, but just as she's thinking this the grand finale begins.

"That's quite a fitting finish to a great day," she says as she looks up into his eyes.

"Yes, pretty spectacular! Don't you think it's about time to be getting the sailboat back to shore? I'm not an accomplished sailor you know."

"You're probably right. I was just enjoying myself too much I guess and don't want the day to end."

"Well, Sam, if you would like, couldn't we spend the night right here on the boat?"

"Oh, Tyler, that would be wonderful. Are you sure you wouldn't mind?"

"No, why would I mind?" He says as he wraps her in his arms and kisses her. With a beautiful woman like you, I'd be foolish to say no."

"Okay, so stay we do," she says as she nudges his neck with her head.

The moon is exceptionally bright tonight and the sky is totally full of stars. They decide to stay out on deck a while longer and enjoy them. Most of the other boats have cleared the area and all that they can see now are the lights of the ones off in the distance that anchored for the night also.

It was getting a little chilly out on the water, so Tyler went below and fetched another blanket.

"Can you see the big dipper, Sam?" He asks as he comes back up on deck.

"Yes, I can," she says as she points to the north and a little west.

He sits back down beside her on the blanket and takes the other one and puts over her. Then he lies back on his elbow and pulls her down beside him.

"Sam, what more could I have asked for? This has been a great day and I have you to thank for it."

"I think it took the two of us didn't it?"

It was early morning when she felt Tyler stir. They'd made love on the deck under the stars, then gone below to bed.

"Good morning," she says as she rolls over and kisses him on the cheek.

"Good morning to you too. What time is it, do you know?"

Turning over to see the clock she sees that it's almost eight o'clock. "It's almost eight why, are you going somewhere?"

"No, I was just asking. What have you got planned for today"

"That's up to you. We can either stay out here on the boat or we can take it in and go spend the day on the beach, and at my place.

"If it's okay with you, why don't we take the sailboat back and spend the day at your place?"

"Okay, let's do."

That's exactly what they did. It took quite a while for them to get the boat back and unpack, so it was nearly eleven when they arrived back at her place. They decided to lie on the beach and maybe take in a swim.

The beach was entirely too crowded, so they decided just to take a walk and come back to the house.

While walking on the beach, Tyler thought he saw some guy watching Samantha a little too closely. Not wanting to say anything to Samantha, he just keeps an eye on him. That looks an awful lot like someone he's seen in town lately. "Sam, what do you say we head back towards your house and sit awhile on the back porch? We can watch the people and the water sports. I enjoy watching them parasail."

"Fine, I'm getting a little tired anyway." Tyler takes her hand and they head back home. They have a leisurely walk back dodging all of the people on the beach. There isn't too much of the beach that isn't covered with people, their chairs, coolers, etc.

They have a very pleasant afternoon sitting on her porch in the swing. Of course Tyler is enjoying all of the females in their skimpy bathing suits just a little too much and she made it a point to rib him continuously about it. She didn't get jealous like she thought she would. She's feeling rather comfortable with their relationship and doesn't see a need to be jealous. He seems very attentive towards her and she thinks he's beginning to really care. She has never experienced a relationship quite like this one and it is starting to feel good. She only hopes he is sincere and isn't just using her while he's in town. Somehow, she doesn't feel that he is, and hopes she's right.

"Sam, are you getting hungry?" He asks her as he pulls her out of her thoughts.

"I could eat something. I can go in and fix us a little something if you'd like."

"No, I don't want you to go to any more trouble for me. Why don't I call and order a pizza and we can stay right here?"

"That's fine, but I don't mind fixing us something." She no sooner says it and he's off the swing headed into the house to phone in the order.

"That was a good idea Tyler. The pizza hit the spot."

"Yes, I enjoyed it too. But, Sam, I think I need to be going," He says as he gets up out of his chair and pulls her out of hers. He puts his arms on her shoulders and pulls her close to him. "Sam, this has been a wonderful weekend and I've enjoyed spending this time with you." He lifts her chin up with his fingers, looks into her eyes and kisses her. She feels a tingling sensation all the way to her toes. "I hope you know what you've come to mean to me. I don't have a clue where this relationship is heading, but I'd like to find out."

"I hope it isn't moving too fast for either one of us," he says as he's still holding her in his arms.

"Why don't we just take it as it comes, Tyler? Do you have to leave so soon?" She asks laying her head on his chest.

"Yes, Sam, I think I'd better. If I don't leave now I'm afraid I'll stay the night and we both have to go to work in the morning."

"That wouldn't be so bad would it?" She says as she looks up at him guiltily.

"Sam, just what are you suggesting? That I stay and we'll both regret it in the morning when neither one of us will want to report to work? Now wouldn't George just love us? What if I promise that we will mix a little work with pleasure this next week? I know we'll want to still keep us low key, but that doesn't mean we can't see each other socially after work. I know I won't be able to stay away from you too long. Sam."

"I'd like that."

"Then it's settled. I'll see you at work in the morning," he says as he kisses her again and it's hard for either of them to pull away.

"Thanks again, Sam," Tyler says as he's opening the door and gives her another kiss on the cheek as he turns to leave. "Be sure and lock this door after I leave okay? I wouldn't want anyone getting my girl."

"Okay, I will. See you in the morning Tyler," she says as she shuts the door behind him.

Leaving Samantha's, Tyler is thinking about the man who was watching Samantha on the beach. He wishes he could remember who he was and what was he doing watching her. He knows what he saw and he *was* staring at her. He'd better keep an eye on her and he also wants to alert George of this tomorrow morning. He hasn't told him about any of the things that have happened to Sam and now he thinks he had better. She was almost hit at the corner the day when they went for lunch, and again when she was pulling into her driveway.

This may all be coincidental, but he'd better alert him just in case. He may also want to alert Tom and Captain Stewart of the situation.

It's getting late, and Samantha knows she'd better get things put away before she retires for the evening, or she'll have to face it tomorrow after work, when she's dead tired. She was thinking to herself what a wonderful weekend it turned out to be. Spending time with Tyler was even more than she anticipated. He's such a wonderful guy and she hopes their relationship can build on the time they just spent together. If this was any indication of what's to come in the near future, she's definitely looking forward to it.

Chapter Ten

On Monday morning, Tyler arrives at the office long before Samantha, knowing that George will be there, trying to catch up after the long weekend.

"Good Morning, George," Tyler says as he steps in the doorway to George's office.

"Same to you, Tyler. What brings you in so early this morning?"

"George, if you have a little time, I'd like to talk to you before Samantha gets in."

"That's fine. I haven't as much to catch up on as I thought. I pretty much took care of everything before the weekend, but you never know what's lurking at you when you return. Now what is it that you have on your mind?" He asks motioning for Tyler to take a seat.

"Well George, I didn't want this to get out, but I figure it is going to sooner rather than later anyway. I've started seeing Samantha and I've become very fond of her."

"Hell, I had that one figured out a while ago. You know this isn't the smartest thing you two could do, considering the two of you are working on this case together don't you?" Saying without looking up.

"Yes, George, I know and I really tried to prevent it, but damn it, it didn't work. And how did you figure it out anyway?" asking George as he's standing there with his hands in pockets.

"It really wasn't that hard, seeing the way you two look at each other. And I believe I overheard you calling her Sam. If you two were strictly on a professional basis, I hardly think you would call her Sam. But Tyler, you are going to have to be very careful now. You could jeopardize Samantha's and also your own safety if you don't keep your minds on the case during working hours."

"I'm fully aware of that, George, and that brings me to the other thing I wanted to discuss with you. A few of the times I've been with Sam, I mean Samantha, I've felt that someone has been following her. I've seen a man a couple of times myself staring at her and I know I've seen him before. Also, she has had a couple of experiences lately that have me very suspicious. Once, as we were going to lunch after leaving here, a car practically ran her down as she stepped off the curb. Another time, I believe the same vehicle tried to ram her as she was turning in her driveway returning home after work. I feel that whoever it is, is trailing her, after she leaves here."

"First, it's okay if you call her Sam. I kind of like it myself. It sort of fits her. But, if what you are telling me is true, you have to be extremely careful. This may have to do with the case and who killed Courtney."

"I know George, and that's what bothers me the most. I realize Sam's life could be in jeopardy, but I don't want her to know yet what we are thinking. I don't believe she has made the connection and I feel she is safer right now not knowing. If she should find out, I'm afraid she'd try to do something stupid. She's a very intelligent lady, but she also could try to take matters into her own hands, if you know what I mean."

"You're right of course. I'll go along with you right now, but if anything else happens to jeopardize either of your safety, I'll pull both of you off the case. The police and the detectives are very capable of handling this on their own. Do we *understand* each other?"

"Yes, George, I understand completely. I'd like for Sam and I to go to the university where Courtney attended. I have a feeling that there is more there that can help shed some light on this case. As soon as Sam gets in this morning, I'd like for us to make arrangements to leave as soon as possible."

"Okay, I'll let the both of you go on one condition. That the both of you check in with me a few times each day and keep me posted. If there is someone out there that is aware of what you two are up to, he may very well follow you there. And also, if at anytime I feel it isn't safe, the two of you are coming right back here." And thumping on his desk with his knuckles, he stands up.

"Thank you George. You can count on me to take care of Sam. When she comes into work this morning, which should be any time now, I'll tell her what we're going to do, but obviously I'll eliminate what we talked about." Tyler then gets up also.

"If it's okay with the both of you, you can leave in the morning. I'm only going to give you a few days on this, so make your time there worthwhile and do it expediently. I'll want you back here pronto, so I can make sure you are safe." And he walks Tyler out.

"Good morning," Samantha says as Tyler whirls around to see her standing in the doorway. "You two are in bright and early this morning. I thought maybe I'd get an early start after the weekend and it looks as if you two beat me to the punch."

"Good morning to you too, Sam," Tyler says to her turning around.

"Hello, Samantha," George replies. "How was your weekend?" He asks with a sheepish grin on his face.

"What's wrong with you this morning George? You look like the cat that swallowed the canary."

"Tyler was just filling me in on the weekend," and George smiles. "I'll tell you the same thing I told him. I understand what is going on between the two of you, *however*, if at any time it starts to interfere with your job, I'll put my foot down and one or the both of you will be off the case. Do you understand me, Samantha?"

"Way to go Tyler! You couldn't keep it our little secret could you?"

"No, Sam, I thought it best to fill George in on what's going on because we are working on this case together. I didn't feel it was fair to hide it from him. And he suspected it anyway. I also talked with him regarding the two of us going to the university and seeing what we could find out about Courtney."

"Oh you did? Well George, what do you think?"

"I just told Tyler okay. The two of you can leave in the morning."

"Thank you George. Tyler seems to think there is more there that we can find out about Courtney and possibly link us to her killer."

"Both of you be extremely careful and don't try any funny stuff. You are to keep in touch with me daily and update me on the situation," George says as he points his finger at Samantha. "Now the two of you get out of my office. I have work to do. Let me know when you will be leaving in the morning and where you will be staying while you are there."

"Okay George," Tyler says to him. "We'll talk to you before we leave and let you know the particulars. Sam, we need to get on the phone and get some reservations made."

"Will do." Samantha says as she's walking out of George's office.

Samantha made the reservations without any trouble. Tyler was going to spend the morning in his office on some paperwork and getting things in order for their visit to the university. The day flew by, but she pretty much had everything in order in her office to leave in the morning. There was still much to do at home, but she thinks that too wouldn't take long. She needs to pack, water the plants, stop the mail, etc. As she was locking her door to leave Tyler comes up behind her.

"How'd your day go, Sam? Did you manage to get everything in order to leave in the morning?"

"Hi. Yes, I believe I'm ready as I'll ever be. I just need to go home now and get the things done there I need to before we leave. What time do you think we need to leave in the morning?"

"Well, I don't know about you, but I'd like to be on the road by nine. How's that for you?"

"Fine I think, barring any unforeseen problems or last minute things I may have forgotten. Do you have any idea about how long we will be gone?"

"No, Sam, I don't, but I'm hoping maybe this will go quickly and we can be out of there in just a few days."

"Me too. I'll pack accordingly, but I'll also be prepared in case it takes longer."

"Great. How about an early dinner?"

"I'd love to Tyler, but I think I had better pass. I've got a lot to do at home and I'll just grab something when I can, but thanks anyway."

"Well there goes any chance of me spending some time with you this evening."

"I'm sorry, but I think we'll have plenty of time in the next few days. I've got to run now. Are you picking me up in the morning or do you want me to meet you here at the office?"

"Why don't I pick you up so your car won't be at the office and we can drive in together?"

"That's fine. We can meet with George then before we leave."

Tyler looked to see if anyone was watching and leaned down to give her a kiss.

"Are you trying to start office gossip?"

"Yes. That will give them something to talk about while we are gone."

"You are devious. But thanks for the kiss. I'll see you in the morning," she says as she turns and heads down the hall.

When she arrives home she makes a list of the things she needs to do so she wouldn't forget anything. She already has the laundry done, so most of the things she needs to take will only have to be thrown in the suitcase. She'd stopped at the post office on her way home and stopped the mail. Now she needs to water the plants and call her parents to let them know she'll be out of town for a few days.

She hasn't talked with her parents since before the weekend of the Fourth of July. She's sure her mom will be anxious to hear how it went. She dials the number of her aunt's in Florida where they are staying, and her mom answers.

"Hi, Mom, how are you doing?" Samantha asks when her mother answers

"Hi, Samantha. I'm doing fine," she says. "We are having such a great time here, I don't know if we'll ever leave. How are you doing and how was your weekend with Tyler?"

"We had a great time mom. He really is wonderful. I'll have to fill you in on all of the details when you return, but right now I need to let you know my plans."

"Oh, okay honey, what's up?"

"Tyler and I are leaving first thing tomorrow morning to go to the university and try to find out what we can there, if anything, about Courtney. Tyler seems to think it will help, so we're going to give it a try. I just wanted to let you know in case you are trying to get a hold of me while I'm gone."

"Thanks for calling honey, and please be careful."

"Okay, Mom, we will. I'll call you from there and keep in touch. Enjoy the rest of your vacation, give dad a hug for me and I'll talk to you in a day or two."

"Bye, Samantha, we love you and please be careful."

"Thanks, Mom. I love you, too; bye." It was one more thing on her to do list she could mark off.

She hasn't eaten much today so she takes time to fix a frozen pizza. She's pretty much ready to go now and she's ready to take a break. When the pizza's done, she fixes a cold drink and eats her pizza while watching a little TV. Before she knows it, she's fallen asleep on the couch in the sitting position and doesn't wake up till after eleven and the news is on. "Damn it! Why did I let myself do that?" She takes a few moments to wake up completely, then gets up, turns off the TV and stumbles to her bedroom.

Chapter Eleven

It's seven o'clock when she hears her alarm go off. She lies there a few minutes and collects her thoughts before she manages to get up. This is going to be quite a task for the two of them to undertake in the next few days. She only hopes for Courtney's sake, that they can uncover something that will help them. Right now any information that they can come up with will be beneficial. She rolls over to get out of bed and the phone rings.

"Good morning, Sam."

"Good morning, Tyler. Why are you calling me so early this morning?"

"I just wanted to make sure that you don't oversleep this morning and we get on the road on time."

"Oh aren't you the sweet one this morning. Yes, I just woke up and I'll be ready when you arrive, thank you very much!"

"Okay, I was just making sure. I'll let you go then and see you at nine."

"Bye, see you then." She knows they will continually give her a rough time for being late that one morning.

Tyler is knocking on her door promptly at nine o'clock and she's ready to go. They put her things in his car and are on the road in due time.

"What do you think, Sam? Are you up to doing this? I just have a gut feeling that we are heading in the right direction. There was just something in talking with Courtney's parents and Sara, that there has to be more to her than even they know, or are not revealing. That girl could *not* have been a saint. I just know it."

"What makes you so sure of that?"

"I went to college myself and so did you. You may or may not have been a perfect little girl at home, but my bet is, when you got to college you spread your wings, and it is my assumption that Courtney did also. I may be way off on this, but somehow I don't think so. Someone killed her and we need to know who and why, and I believe our answer is at the university."

"You may be right, but who and why did it happen? I don't understand what she could have done and why anyone would want to kill her."

The drive to the university was pretty quiet. Both Tyler and Samantha had thoughts of their own and were concentrating on what approach to take once they were there. Neither one of them notices the black SUV following them, yet.

"Sam, I'm getting pretty hungry, how about you? I noticed at the next exit there are quite a few eating-places. Want to stop for a bite to eat and stretch our legs?"

"Yeah, sure. I didn't take time to eat this morning and I am a little hungry."

Tyler takes the next exit and comes to the stop sign. Where would you like to eat?

"There are a couple fast food places, a Pizza Hut and Steak 'n Shake. Pick one."

"How about Steak 'n Shake? I love their fries and steak burgers."

"Sounds good to me. I'd like to get out and stretch my legs and take a break."

As Tyler's turning onto the frontage road that took them to the entrance of the Steak 'n Shake, he thinks he sees a black SUV close behind them. Remembering the past few weeks of seeing a black SUV and Sam's experiences, his antenna goes up when it comes to SUV's. It may be a coincidence, but nevertheless he'd better keep his eyes open. No need to alarm Sam, though. She wasn't too optimistic about this trip anyway and he doesn't want to scare her for no reason. If at the point he needs to alert her, he will do so, but in the meantime he doesn't want her worrying.

Pulling into a Steak 'n Shake parking spot and getting out of the car, Tyler looks around to see if he can spot the SUV. He doesn't see one. At least not parked where he can see it or if there even was one. He may be getting a little paranoid at this point and imagining things. He sure hopes so, for both their sakes.

"I'm starved," Samantha remarks, as she closes the door. "Their fries and a steak burger sound great right now."

"Then let's go in and eat," Tyler says as he takes her hand and enters the restaurant. "We only have about an hour and a half left before we reach the university once we leave here."

Both Tyler and Samantha have their professional faces on. Their personal relationship has been left back at Palmetto for the time being. They are too much into where they are going and for what, to let their relationship enter now.

It's almost three o'clock when they arrive at the motel. They didn't have any trouble locating it, knowing it was near the university and they already knew where that was, so finding the motel didn't take long.

Samantha had been thinking during the drive what kind of sleeping arrangements Tyler would want. When making the reservations she didn't want to be presumptuous, so she reserved two rooms. She hadn't mentioned this to him and she wonders what he will think of the idea. She would soon find out.

Approaching the counter, Samantha takes the initiative and speaks with the motel clerk first since she'd made the reservations before they left.

"May I help you?" The motel clerk asks.

He's a nice looking young man and she knows this is going to be awkward for him once Tyler learns of the arrangements.

"Yes, you may." Samantha answers. "I'm Samantha Summers, and I believe we have reservations."

"Samantha Summers. Would you mind spelling the last name for me please?" The motel clerk asks.

"Of course not, S-u-m-m-e-r-s."

"Thank you," the clerk says and enters the correct spelling into the computer.

"I have you for two non-smoking rooms with queen size beds, correct?"

"Yes, I believe that is correct," Samantha says as she looks over at Tyler.

"Sam, may I have a word with you please?" Tyler asks.

Tyler grabs Samantha by the elbow and pulls her away from the counter as not to let the clerk hear what he is about to say to her.

"Samantha, what are you doing? I assumed we'd be rooming together. Is there something wrong?"

"No, I didn't know when I was making the reservations what your preference would be, so I played it safe and got separate rooms. I didn't want to be presumptuous!"

"Well, as far as I'm concerned you can change these two rooms into *one* room, that is if you don't mind."

"I'm sorry. I knew we were coming here on a professional basis and I thought I was doing the right thing. If we were keeping this strictly business, I didn't want to complicate matters."

Samantha looks up at Tyler, smiles and then turns to return to the counter.

The clerk is typing on the computer when Samantha approaches and pretends like he hadn't heard their conversation, even though he had heard most of it and was smiling. Lucky guy he thought. Nice girl too, not getting the room together and not being easy.

"If you don't mind sir, could we change that to one room instead of two?" Samantha asks thinking what shade of red her face must be right now.

"Of course, it's no trouble. One room with a queen size bed it is then, unless you'd like to change that to a king," the clerk states.

"Yes, thank you. One king will be fine," Samantha says smiling up at Tyler who is now standing beside her.

"How many nights will you be staying?" The clerk asks.

"Could we leave that end open?" Asks Tyler.

"Sure, that will be fine," says the clerk. "Just let me know the morning you are going to check out so I can have your paperwork ready to make your check out easier."

The clerk handed them two room key cards, thanked them and told them to have a nice stay, and if there was anything they needed just to call down to the desk.

As they were leaving the lobby the clerk thought how lucky of a guy the gentleman was to have such a nice pretty girl with him. He thought they made a nice couple.

Tyler looked down at Samantha as they were exiting the motel to retrieve their luggage, wondering what she really thought about the sleeping arrangements but electing not to say anything until they were in their room.

"Sam, I'll get the luggage if you'll get our briefcases from the backseat. I think our room is close enough from here that we can use the elevator in the lobby. Then I'll come back down and park the car."

"Okay, I think you're right."

Opening the door to the room Samantha notices the décor first. She particularly likes the choice of spread on the king size bed which is located on the left side, right past the bathroom that is also on the left, as they enter the room. It's a floral pastel in yellows, pinks and soft greens. The room is painted a light green to coordinate with the spread and the curtain that covers the sliding glass door matches the spread. There is a round table and two armchairs directly in front of the sliding glass door with a lamp hovering over the table.

Once in the room they both rid themselves of what they carried. Tyler notices that Sam seems uncomfortable.

"Are you okay with this arrangement, Sam? If not, I can get my own room."

"No, it's fine really. I just feel a little uncomfortable that's all."

"Why don't I go down to the lounge and have a drink while you're unpacking. Maybe that will make you feel a little at ease?"

"I'd hate for you to do that, but if you don't mind maybe that would be best."

"Fine. I'll be back in a little while." And he heads for the lounge.

There are double dressers up against the wall opposite the bed, so Samantha uses the dresser on the left for her clothes.

Once she's unpacked and has all of her personal belongings put away, she realizes how foolish she's been and decides to go down and get Tyler. She shouldn't have reacted in that manner; after all they did spend time on the boat over the 4th.

When she reaches the lounge she spots Tyler sitting up at the bar. It's still pretty early and not many people are in the lounge. It's fairly dark just like most bars, but has a little atmosphere.

Walking up to Tyler she lifts herself up onto the barstool beside him. "I'm sorry Tyler. I shouldn't have reacted that way. I don't know what got into me. I think this whole thing is a little unsettling. But thank you for giving me time to get myself together."

"Would you like a drink?"

"What are you having?"

"I'm having a bourbon and water."

"I think I'll have a wine-spritzer."

"Bartender, the lady here would like a wine-spritzer please."

Tyler takes a look at Sam and sees that she is still a little nervous. "Sam, can we talk about this? I can see that you are still uneasy. Why don't we move over there to a booth where we can talk?"

As the bartender brings Samantha her drink they move to the nearest booth.

Chapter Twelve

He decides to pick a motel across the street and down about a block, as not to be too close to where Samantha is staying, but doesn't want to be so far away that he can't keep his eye on her. He'd get a room in front if he could, to be able to watch her coming and going.

When he'd followed them out of Palmetto he had no clue as to where they were headed until they were almost there. He didn't think that they had seen him follow them, but he wasn't sure and he couldn't stay in the same motel and risk the chance of her spotting him. He was going to keep his distance and see why they are here and what they are after.

He's been following both of them since this guy came to town and he isn't happy that He's spending so much time with Samantha. It seems that everywhere she is, he isn't far behind. Getting rid of her before she can discover too much information on who had killed Courtney isn't going to be as easy as he had first thought. If she'd worked alone on the case it would have been simple, but now that she has this guy working with her and he seldom lets her out of his sight, stopping her isn't going to be as easy as he thought. He knows she is good and now that there were two of them, he has to dispose of Samantha before she gets too close. And if she starts snooping around the university and asks too many questions, someone is going to bring his name into it and then Samantha will fit the pieces together.

He checks into the motel and is able to get the room he wants. He tries to park his SUV where it can't be spotted. If they notice him and catch his license plates, he can't afford for them to spot the SUV at the motel.

They would put two and two together with the times he'd tried to run Samantha down, and his chances of getting rid of her would vanish.

His room isn't the greatest, but he isn't planning to be here long and it is the best place to stay and be able to watch her. He hasn't brought anything with him because he didn't know where they were headed and why, but he knew he had to follow. He could pick up a few things he'd need and make do.

Sitting down on his king-size bed he picks up the TV remote control and hits the power button to turn on the TV. He figures they'll be in the motel for the evening after the drive here, so he won't have to follow them till morning. He is going to have to have a strategy and get rid of her fast.

Tyler and Samantha leave the lounge after she finished her spritzer and feels a little more at ease about the situation once they had talked. What they don't notice as they are leaving, is the gentleman sitting in the corner watching them. He'd decided sitting in the motel waiting for morning isn't getting him anywhere. He needs to see where their rooms are and keep as close a watch on them as he can. As they approach the elevator he can see from where he is sitting the floor level numbers and will be able to tell which floor they got off on. Once they reach their floor, he can take the stairs and hopefully get to their floor in time to see which room is hers.

He sees that they get off on the fourth floor, so he runs to the door that leads to the stairs and hopes he can get to the fourth floor in time to see which room number she enters. He's just opening the door on the fourth floor as he sees her walk into the room. He walks to the door noting that the room number on the door is four ten. While making mental note of the number, he puts his ear to the door to see if he can make out anything they are saying but can't. He has no way of knowing whether this is her room or his, or even if they have one room together. He could hang around a little longer and see if she'll come out, but he would look pretty suspicious if anyone else sees him wondering around seemingly with no where to go. He decides the best bet would be to go back to his motel till morning and then follow them and make his move the first chance he gets.

Entering the room Tyler knows that Sam feels more comfortable with the arrangements now. As she enters the room behind Tyler she shuts the door and turns the lock. Tyler hasn't unpacked, so he proceeds to do so. She takes the remote control off the top of the TV that is located inside the armoire and turns it on, thinking she can catch up on the news while Tyler unpacks and sits down on the edge of the bed. Knowing they aren't planning on being there but a couple of days, it will take him no time to unpack.

After hanging up his shirts, he walks over to Sam, takes the remote out of her hand, pulls her up off the bed and put his arms around her waist.

"Feel better now, Sam?" He asks as he kisses her on the forehead.

"I do now. Thanks for being patient with me," she says as she rests her head in the crook of his neck.

At that moment he starts pulling her t-shirt out of her slacks. Not knowing what her reaction might be, he's taking a big chance, but he wants to show her just how much she means to him. Knowing full well what they were doing here, he knew he was taking a chance of rejection, but he's going to give it a try. He hasn't felt this way about anyone in a long time, if ever, and he isn't going to lose her.

"Tyler," she says in a low voice, looking into his eyes as her heart starts to beat faster.

Looking into her eyes while pulling the shirt up over her breasts he says, "Sam, I know you think this is too soon, but I'm falling in love with you. I blew it once before and I'm not going to do it again. I've never felt quite like this with anyone before and I'm not going to take the chance of losing you by not telling you so."

"I think I know what you mean. I just feel that we were meant to be. Maybe this is why I'm so nervous. Being here with you feels right."

He continues to slip her shirt over her head as she starts to unbutton his. Both of their pulses start to race as they undress each other. They're falling onto the king-sized bed almost before they've finished undressing. He's kissing her all over as he rolls her over and is sitting on top of her. Looking up at him with a lot of passion in her eyes, she puts her arms around his neck and pulls him down on top of her and kisses him. He uses his knee to spread her legs to enter her as he puts her arms up over her head. She starts to move in rhythm with him and in no time they are both ready.

"Slow down, Sam," he whispers in her ear. "I want us to enjoy this as long as we can."

But it doesn't last long. Neither one of them can hold back. They climax at the same time. Tyler holds her tight around her buttocks until her legs fall limp around him. Then moving her hair out of her eyes, he falls limp on top of her.

"I love you," she says as she's smiling back up at him and completely spent herself.

He rolls off of her, lies down beside her and pulls her into his arms. "I love you too," he says as his finger circles her face. "I can't explain how this has happened so fast but maybe there isn't to be any explanation."

"I know. It's just happened."

Chapter Thirteen

Before they know it, it's morning and the telephone ringing awakens them. They'd left a wake up call with the desk clerk when they checked in. She rolls over, picks up the phone and hears the voice recording giving them the time. Hanging up the receiver she lies back down and finds Tyler resting on his elbow looking at her with a big smile on his face.

"Good morning," he says as he pulls her over to him and kisses her. "I love you."

"Good morning. I love you too," she says as she gives him a hug.

"Let's not forget last night, Sam. I want to stay here, but we both know we have a job to do and we'd better get started."

Tyler knows by now they have completely forgotten that this is strictly a business venture and he should not mix pleasure with business. If this would prove costly to them later is yet to be seen. He would have to be very careful as not to let it get in the way of their investigation. He is sure George wouldn't be very proud of him about now. He'd promised him he wouldn't let this happen.

It's nine o'clock and he hasn't seen them come out of the motel yet. He's getting a little impatient with them. He's guessing, but he thought Samantha and that guy were staying in the same room last night. Just what did they have going on anyway? He asks. It just makes things a little more complicated. No wonder he didn't let her out of his sight long, when they were in Palmetto. He thought maybe he was protecting her, but now he knows there is more to it. He is going to have to make his move fast and get out of here.

Tyler and Sam eat breakfast in the motel restaurant. They know they can't possibly talk with anyone at the university until after nine, so they aren't in a hurry. After last night both of them are starved. Over breakfast they discuss their plan for the day and know the first place they will head will be the personnel office.

Leaving the motel restaurant, they head for the university. They have no trouble at all locating the personnel office and once there they ask to speak to the personnel director.

Both Tyler and Sam introduce themselves to the personnel director, Bob Jameson, and explain why they are there. Mr. Jameson tells them he'd read about Courtney and knew she was a graduate of the university. He also tells them that after he'd read about her, he'd starting checking into her background there in case someone came around asking questions.

"Would you mind giving us the names of some of her professors and the library personnel?" Tyler asks.

"I'll be glad to. In fact, I've already done some research on my own," he says as he reaches down to open a drawer and pulls out a manila folder and hands it to Tyler.

"Courtney and I went to high school together Mr. Jameson. I have a personal reason to want to get to the bottom of this and find who killed her. It's just a coincidence that I also happen to be an investigative reporter for the *Carolina Tribune*."

"I see," Mr. Jefferson states. "You both know then that if anyone from a detective's office comes and asks for the same information, I must give it to them also. I can't believe they haven't been here asking already." Tyler's looks over the folder and finds that Mr. Jameson has a complete list of just about all of the university personnel that Courtney may have come in contact with. "Thank you very much Mr. Jameson," he says. "If you don't mind I believe we need to get started."

"No, that's fine," Mr. Jameson says as he's getting out of his chair, coming around the desk and shakes hands with both Tyler and Sam. He tells them the easiest way to get to the university library and then shows them to the door.

"Thank you so much, Mr. Jameson," Samantha says as she's leaving his office.

"If you need me for anything else, please do not hesitate to call me," he says as he's reaching into his pocket, pulling out his business card and hands it to Tyler. "I'm sure my personnel will be as helpful as they can."

"Good bye Mr. Jameson," Tyler says as they both walk out towards the front of the personnel office.

"That was easy," Tyler says as they head down the steps to his car.

"Let's hope the rest is as easy," Sam says. "But for some reason I don't think that it will be the case. Courtney was such a quiet girl."

"Remember what I said, I still have this hunch she was an entirely different person while she was here."

"Well let's get started. The sooner we are out of here the better I will feel," Sam says when a little chill runs down her spine. Shaking if off she follows Tyler to the car.

He's sitting in his SUV watching for them as they come out of the personnel office. Being careful that Samantha doesn't spot him, he slumps down into the seat so he is just barely able to see over the dashboard. It's pretty warm this morning and he left his vehicle running so he can have the air-conditioning on. He wishes he'd put on his shorts, but he didn't know what situation would arise and if he was going to be able to get Samantha today, he wanted to be ready for anything. Shorts would not be the correct attire for the dirty work. He isn't worried that Tyler will spot the SUV. He was very careful in following them and kept a reasonable distance for that very reason. Besides, there are enough vehicles in the immediate area that he shouldn't be spotted. He is probably being a little paranoid.

The library is located on the other side of campus, so they decide to drive over rather than walk. It's a rather warm morning anyway and they don't know their way around. Tyler opens the door for Samantha and she climbs in. Shutting the door he goes around the back of the car to get into his side. Getting behind the wheel he looks at Samantha and winks.

"Are you ready for this, Sam?" He asks as he shuts his door and puts the key in the ignition. "Let's get this over with so we can get back to Palmetto," he says as he grabs her hand and squeezes it.

"I'm ready as I'll ever be. I only hope this proves to be beneficial."

Tyler pulls out of the parking space and drives to the library. It's not that far from the personnel office. Pulling up to the front of the library, Tyler puts the car in park to let Samantha out.

"I'll let you out and I'll go park in the parking lot. I see there is a fifteen-minute parking limit here. Go on in and I'll be right there."

"Okay, thanks," Samantha says as she opens her door to let herself out.

She no sooner gets inside than Tyler's right behind her. "I need to use the little girl's room," she says to him as he comes up beside her and she's pointing to the sign that's to the right.

"Okay, I'll wait right here for you," he says as he sets down on an old wooden bench in the foyer. He notices the library is very old. He can tell it has been renovated, but that they'd kept most of its old charm. He's thinking how nice of them to do so. Anymore, they tear down the old buildings and replace them with new modern ones and don't care about their history.

He parks his SUV in the same parking lot, gets out of the car and proceeds to the entrance of the library. Thinking that they were a few minutes ahead of him he enters the library just as Samantha is coming out of the ladies restroom. Hoping she hasn't spotted him he ducks back out the front door. He thinks he's safe because as she's coming out the door she's looking down replacing her belt in the loop on her slacks. "That was really a close call," he mumbles. If the gentleman with Samantha sees him he wouldn't recognize him. He doesn't know him anyway. He'll just wait out on the front steps a few minutes until they have time to get out of his sight. He's pretty sure if they come to the library, he knows what they are up to. This isn't going to be easy. The librarian will definitely know who he is and he can't let her or Amanda (Courtney's college friend), see him, but he has to keep a close eye on Samantha. She's getting too close and he knows it's just a matter of time before she knows the truth. She won't be able to immediately connect him to the murder, but she's too sharp a lady not to eventually figure that out too. He's going to have to work fast now. Time is of the essence.

"Okay, I'm ready Tyler," Samantha says as she's coming out of the restroom smoothing down the front of her slacks after she's finished buckling them.

"Good let's go locate Mrs. Appleby," Tyler says as he gets up off the bench.

Approaching the front desk Tyler sees a pretty young lady, obviously a college student working over the summer, behind it.

"Good morning miss," Tyler says to her as he reaches the counter. " We are here to see Christina Appleby. Is she in this morning?"

"Yes, she is," the young lady says to him. "May I tell her who is here to see her?"

"My name is Mr. Tyler Worth and this is Miss Samantha Summers," Tyler says as he looks at Samantha and reaches into his shirt pocket to get out one of his business cards to hand to her.

"We work for the *Carolina Tribune* out of Palmetto."

"Thank you." The young lady says. "Excuse me while I go get her."

The young lady proceeds to the backroom to retrieve Mrs. Appleby.

"Mrs. Appleby?" She inquires. "Are you back here? There is someone here to see you."

"Yes, I'm back here, Amanda. Who is it that wants to see me?" She asks.

"It's is a Mr. Tyler Worth and a Miss Samantha Summers from the *Carolina*

Tribune in Palmetto," She says as she hands her Tyler's business card.

"Oh my." She says. "I'll bet they are here about Courtney. I wondered how long it would take for someone to come poking around here. Tell them I'll be right out Amanda."

"Mrs. Appleby," she says. "I'm sure if they knew that Courtney and I were roommates they'd want to talk to me too."

"Did you tell them who you are?" Mrs. Appleby asks.

"No, they didn't ask me my name, they were just asking for you."

"Well after I talk with them I'll tell them about you, Amanda, and I'm sure they will have more questions to ask you than me."

"I know. I thought I recognized her from Courtney's funeral. She looks a little familiar."

"Will you cover for me while I talk to them in my office, Amanda?"

"Sure." Amanda says as she walks with Mrs. Appleby to the front desk.

"I'm Mrs. Christina Appleby," she says as she extends her hand to shake hands with Tyler and Samantha. "Amanda tells me you are from the *Carolina Tribune* and have some questions for me regarding Courtney."

"Yes, we do, Mrs. Appleby." Tyler says as he shakes her hand. "This is Samantha Summers and she is the one that works for the *Carolina Tribune*. I'm not from Palmetto, but I'm down from Pittsburgh to help her on the case."

"Hello, Mrs. Appleby." Samantha says. "Pleased to meet you. If you don't mind we would like to ask you a few questions."

"That's fine. Please come with me. I'll take you to my office where we can have some privacy."

The library isn't full, but it does have summer college students in here and some of them are sitting pretty close to the front desk.

Opening her office door, Christina asks Tyler and Samantha to be seated. Going to her little refrigerator behind her desk to get out a cold drink, she asks them if they'd care for anything.

"No, thank you." Tyler and Samantha say simultaneously.

"Mrs. Appleby, could you describe what kind of person Courtney was during her employment here at the library?" Tyler asks.

Pulling out her chair and being seated, Mrs. Appleby says. "First of all, please call me Christina. I became very close to Courtney the four years she was a student here at the university. She came seeking a library position her freshman year. I don't normally hire them their first year here. It's enough just getting use to the change from leaving home, the new surroundings and studies, let alone trying to hold down a job too. But Courtney was so sharp and knowledgeable about the library system, that I couldn't turn her down. With her knowledge it was very easy for the students to ask for her assistance. They knew if they needed any references Courtney would be more than happy to help them and she'd know exactly where to go to find the materials or point them in the right direction. An awful lot of the students were on a first name basis with her."

"Christina, do you know if Courtney was seeing anyone while she was here?" Tyler asks.

"Yes, I think she was. There was a young man that would come in here quite frequently to see her. Let me see if I can recall his name," she says as she pushes her glasses back up on the bridge of her nose. "I think his name was Jacob. But I'm sorry I don't recall his last name. The one person that would know his name and can probably tell you all the details is Amanda, the young lady you met at the front desk."

"Amanda you said?" Courtney asks. "Then correct me if I'm wrong, but was she Courtney's roommate?"

"Yes, she was," Christina replies. "They were very close. In fact I just told her that you would most likely prefer to talk with her more than me."

"If you don't mind, Christina, we'd like to ask you a few more questions before we get to Amanda," Tyler says. "You probably aren't aware of this, but Courtney was a very, shall we say, shy person when she was back home and kept pretty much to herself. Did she come across at all like that to you while she was here working?"

"Heavens no!" Christina exclaims. "Courtney was a little shy when she first started here, but in no time it was like she'd worked here forever. She was a very likeable outgoing person, with a great personality. That was one of the reasons I liked her so much. Most of the students that come in for the first time are very apprehensive and aren't quite sure how to ask for what they are looking for. Courtney made them feel very at ease and in no time they became very accustomed to our library system. A lot of them became good friends with her. At the end of her shift on many occasions there would be several students waiting for her. It would be very hard for me to believe that she was just the opposite when she was at home.

"Christina, I have this theory that whoever she was with while she was here whether it was her boyfriend or not, that someone was the one that killed her. Why, we don't know, but I'll tell you this, we aim to find out," Tyler remarks while glancing over at Samantha and seeing the disbelief on her face.

"Oh Mr. Worth, are you sure?" Christina asks. "It didn't seem to me she had an enemy in the world. She was such a likeable young lady."

"We are not sure of anything at this point Christina," Samantha says. "We are just trying to sort this out. Even though I work for the *Tribune*, I was also a friend of Courtney's. We went to high school together and were in the same class. It is hard for me to believe that we are talking about the same person. Courtney always kept to herself. She'd dress down as not to attract attention from the boys and would never have heard of being out running around with the rest of us. Something must have really changed her when she left home and came here to college. Then when she graduated and returned to Palmetto she went to work for the library there. We couldn't believe with her intelligence that she'd come back to Palmetto when her opportunities out there would have been endless. It just doesn't make sense."

"I'm sorry," Christina says. "Maybe I should bring Amanda in now and you can question her. She should be able to shed a lot of light on this for you."

"Thank you, Christina, you have been a great help," Tyler says. "If you think of anything else please contact us. We will most likely be in town a few days."

Tyler told her where they were staying and their room number.

Christina gets up from behind her desk and goes over to the door. "I'll get Amanda. Is there anything I can get either of you?"

"If you don't mind, I'd like a soda now," Samantha says.

"Sure, help yourself," she says as she points to her refrigerator. "I'll be right back."

Tyler stands up when Amanda comes through the door. "Hello, Amanda. I believe we met out front."

"Yes we did," she says. "Mrs. Appleby said you might have some questions for me." She says as she pulls a chair out and sits down.

"Amanda, weren't you Courtney's roommate while she was here?" Samantha asks.

"Yes, I was. I knew when you walked in that I'd seen you somewhere, but I couldn't recall where. Now I know that I saw you at Courtney's funeral, didn't I?"

"Yes, you probably did. It was such a huge funeral I'm afraid I don't recall seeing you," Samantha says.

"How are Courtney's parents doing?" Amanda asks. "I feel so sorry for them. I'd stayed at their home a few times when I'd go home on weekends occasionally with Courtney. They are such nice people."

"Amanda, did you ever see a difference in Courtney's behavior when you would go home on weekends with her?" Tyler asks.

"Yes, I did notice a couple things." Amanda says. "She was always quieter and dressed pretty conservatively while she was home, compared to how she was and how she dressed while at school. I never thought much about it, though. I just figured maybe her parents were very religious and Courtney was trying to please them. She never said anything, and I didn't intrude."

"I'm starting to think she had a split personality Amanda. It seems to me that she was two different people, one when she was home and then the other when she was here. Why, we don't know," Tyler explains. "Did Courtney have a boyfriend while she was here, or was she seeing someone?"

"Yes." Amanda says. "She had a boyfriend. They'd just started going out her senior year. Most of the time we would just be in a group hanging out together then Courtney started dating Jacob and they became very close."

"You say his name was Jacob?" Samantha asks, getting a little nervous. "What was his last name, if you don't mind me asking."

"His last name was I believe, Benzing," she says.

"*Jacob Benzing?*" Samantha cries. "*Are you absolutely sure?*"

"Yes, I am. Are you all right Miss Summers? You suddenly look awfully pale?"

"Samantha, what's wrong?" Tyler asks as he also sees that she has become very pale. "Are you okay?"

"I need a minute Tyler," she says.

Thinking quickly Tyler asks. "Samantha, what did you say your ex-boyfriend's name was?"

"Jacob." Samantha says. "But I never told you what his last name was. It's Benzing. Tyler, what is going on here? Am I hearing that my Jacob and Courtney's Jacob are one and the same person?"

"I don't know, Sam, but from what I'm hearing I believe so. When did things start going awry with you and Jacob? Could Courtney have been the reason that you two broke up? Was Jacob the reason that Courtney came back to Palmetto? Sam, help me out here," he says moving closer and putting his arm around her.

"Would you two like for me to leave you alone for a few minutes to sort this out?" Amanda asks. "I need to check in with Mrs. Appleby anyway, if you are going to need me much longer and see if she can cover for me the rest of the day. I believe we have a lot to talk about."

"Sure Amanda. Why don't you do that? I believe we need some time here, thank you," Tyler says.

Once Amanda leaves the office, Samantha breaks down.

"Sam, we've got to put this together and fast. Do you know what implications this has? If Jacob is one and the same person, this just became very dangerous. If he knows you are working on the case and even remotely suspects you are getting anywhere close to him, you are in danger."

"Tyler what makes you think he has anything to do with Courtney's death?" Sam asks sobbing.

"Think about it.

Did you see Jacob at Courtney's funeral? You never mentioned to me that he was there, was he?"

"No, he wasn't."

"And Courtney's parents didn't even know he existed. Why not Sam? Tyler asks still holding onto Sam.

Tyler's head spinning, he just thinks of something. "Sam, remember the black SUV that almost ran you down at the corner? Did that look anything like Jacob?"

"I didn't see the driver it happened so fast."

"How about when you drove home that evening and the same black SUV almost rammed you? Did you see the person then?"

"*No!*" She exclaims. It was already past me and all I could see was the back of someone's head."

"Sam, I didn't tell you this, but when we were walking on the beach over the Fourth, I observed someone staring at you. I didn't connect at the time, but I now believe it was the same guy that was across the street when we went out to eat that day, and you said it was Jacob, your ex-boyfriend. Sam, why did you two breakup?"

"Oh God, Tyler," she says. "What is going on? Why would he want to kill Courtney if he was in love with her?"

"I don't have any answers, but I think we need to call George and tell him what is going on. Also we need to ask Amanda a few more questions. She probably knows more than she's had time to tell us. Are you going to be all right?"

"Yes, I'll be okay. This is such a shock. Do you think Courtney knew he was going with me also?"

"I'm not sure, but I think that might be the reason things went bad. Courtney probably found out he was going with you and things got ugly. I'm just guessing at this point, but I'll bet she either saw the two of you together or someone did and told her. He broke off with you but that wasn't enough. She felt betrayed, and then he had lost you both. He couldn't handle it and took it out on her. Sam, I need to call George. We need someone to put a tail on Jacob."

Tyler was sure Mrs. Appleby wouldn't mind if he uses her phone. He pulls George's business card out of his wallet and dials the number that directly rings in his office.

"Chambliss here," George says when he answers his phone.

"George, it's Tyler. Have you got a few minutes?"

"Sure Tyler, what's up?" He asks. "Is everything okay with you and Samantha?"

"No, George it's not," Tyler remarks. "We are in the university library now and we are speaking with Courtney's roommate, Amanda Jeffers. She has some rather interesting news for us."

"Okay, go on," George says. "I'm listening."

"Amanda says that Courtney was having a relationship with a guy by the name of Jacob Benzing."

"So, what are you trying to tell me?" George inquires.

"Jacob Benzing is Samantha's ex-boyfriend. Apparently he was going with both of the girls at the same time. My theory is, Courtney found out about Samantha, who is a good friend of Courtney's and approached Jacob and then things got out of hand from then on. He broke it off with Samantha and wanted to stay with Courtney, but Courtney didn't like the idea of betraying her friend and confronted Jacob. At that point, who knows. I don't think Sam knew why their relationship went awry. He never really had a good explanation. That's why it was so hard for her."

"Hm. Tyler this could spell trouble for both you and Samantha, as far as that goes."

"Also, George, remember me telling you that I thought someone might be tailing Sam?"

"Yes, I remember."

"George can we get someone on Jacob as soon as possible?" He asks. "I'm afraid for Sam."

"Consider it done. As soon as I know his whereabouts I'll let you two know. In the meantime, be very careful and watch your backs. And Tyler, let Sam know that you suspect that someone was following her. At this point keeping things from her might be more harmful to her."

"I've more or less told her already George," Tyler confesses. "I reminded her about the day she was almost run down in town, and also while she was pulling into her driveway. George, these are not coincidences anymore."

"I'll get back with you as soon as I can, and Tyler, please keep in touch."

"Thank you. I'll talk to you soon."

Tyler hangs up the phone and notices Samantha sitting there just staring into space.

"Sam, George is going to get someone on Jacob ASAP. I wouldn't be surprised though if he is unable to do that. I have a feeling he is probably right here in town watching us. We are going to have to be very careful, Sam,"

"I'm so frightened." Sam says as Tyler moves from around the desk to sit back down by her. "We need to get Amanda back in here and see what else she knows. She may have the answers we are looking for."

About that time the door opens and Amanda walks back in.

"Amanda, I've just talked to George at our office," Tyler says as he pulls the chair back out for her to sit down.

"Yes, and what did he say?" Amanda asks. "He's very concerned and thinks that we are in danger. He's pretty certain that more than likely Jacob has been following Samantha and is probably right here in town keeping an eye on her," he says as he looks down and sees tears streaming down Sam's face.

"Sam, I can see that this is really upsetting you. You obviously had a lot of feelings for this guy and are frightened now too. Maybe we should just get out of here and talk later," Tyler says as he hands Sam his handkerchief.

"Yes. If you don't mind, I really need some fresh air."

"Amanda, would you be able to leave for awhile? I'd like for you to take Sam to your place and get her settled down a little and then maybe the two of you can talk for awhile and learn more about Courtney and Jacob's relationship"

"I don't see that as a problem. I'll explain the situation to my boss and I'm sure she won't mind," Amanda says looking at Tyler with a worried look on her face.

"But what will you do?" Sam asks looking up at him.

"I'm going to remain here and see if I can't spot Jacob. I'll be right behind you."

Chapter Fourteen

"I'm going to have to work fast." Jacob is thinking to as he returns to his SUV and starts the engine. Giving Samantha this much time with Amanda, she would definitely figure this whole thing out, and if not Samantha, then the gentleman with her would.

Jacob thinking and calculating his next move spots Samantha and Amanda descending the stairs at the library. Not wanting the two girls to spot him, he starts the engine and exits the parking lot before they get any closer. He knows where he can go and no one will know his whereabouts. He'll go to the little storage shed behind the football field he'd frequented with Courtney on occasion. It stores old equipment that isn't used anymore and no one ever went there except the two of them. It was their secret rendezvous place where they could be alone.

Parking his SUV behind the shed Jacob gets out and closes the door. He knows where he always kept the key and so did Courtney.

"Yes!" He says as he reaches over the door casing and feels the key. Looking around to make sure no one has seen him, he inserts the key into the keyhole and turns it. "Damn," he says as he turns the key and the door won't open. Shoving on the door does nothing either, so he takes the key out and inserts it again as he's looking around again to see if anyone has spotted him yet. He's getting agitated and is sweating profusely.

Turning the key and leaning on the door the second time, the door opens and he almost falls in. He shuts the door immediately so as not to be seen.

After stumbling through the door, he looks around the shed and notices nothing has changed. The small space he and Courtney had cleared for the two of them was still there and the Indian blanket was still folded on a stack of old football helmets. This brings back memories, and a little grin comes to the corner of his mouth. "What fun we shared here, Courtney," he says aloud. "If only you hadn't found out about my relationship with Samantha, we could still be together. But you had to go and spoil it all, Courtney. Therefore I did what I had to do."

Realizing he's talking aloud he laughs and knows he has to start thinking about his next move. He's going to have to get to Samantha. He knows that Amanda and Samantha left the library by themselves. He'd seen them pull out of the parking lot together and the gentleman was not with them. He'd assumed they'd go to Amanda's apartment. He knows where she lives so he'd better get there and fast. Now that he knows where he can bring Samantha, he'll leave the shed door unlocked and go get her. Knowing this isn't going to be easy, he's thinking of a plan on the way to Amanda's apartment.

As Tyler's leaving the library to follow close behind the two girls, Christina spots him and starts talking. "Mr. Worth," she says. "If there is anything else I can do for you would you please let me know? We all thought the world of Courtney."

"Thank you, Christina," Tyler says, as he's anxious to leave. "Right now I need to be as close to Samantha and Amanda as I can. If this guy is anywhere near this university, I don't want him to see them alone. I must hurry, but thanks for everything," he says as he opens the front door to the library.

Running down the front library stairs Tyler is looking for the two girls. "Shit!" He doesn't see the girls in the parking lot. The parking lot was almost bare when they arrived and there aren't many cars in the parking lot now and they definitely aren't in one of them.

"I've got to hurry and catch up with them." Tyler exclaims under his breath. "If Jacob is here, I don't want him to see them alone. It's hard telling what he might do." Turning out onto the main road, he's trying to remember the directions to Amanda's apartment. He knows he has to go a few blocks then turn right at the stoplight and her apartment complex is on the right, just one more block down on the left. He remembers the remaining directions to Amanda's apartment once he enters the front gate.

Shutting the door to the shed, Jacob hurries to his SUV to get to Samantha before *he* does.

Whoever this guy is and whatever his name, doesn't matter to him. Samantha is going to be his!

Jacob speeds as fast as he can to Amanda's apartment hoping he won't get stopped by the police. Pulling up in front of Amanda's apartment he doesn't see the car that Samantha rode in with the gentleman to the university. "Yes," he says too. "She's mine!"

Jumping out of his SUV, Jacob slowly walks to the side of Amanda's apartment to see if he can see in the window on the north. He knows the layout of her apartment from being there several times with Courtney, and that he can see into the TV room from this side. With any luck at all the girls will be in that room. Crouching low under the window so as not to be spotted by the girls, he slowly eases up to peek into the window. Samantha and Amanda are both in the TV room. Amanda has her back to him but he can see Samantha's face and he can tell she's crying. He's unable to hear any of their conversation, but doesn't really care. He starts walking around the other side of her apartment to see if he can get in the back door to the kitchen.

Reaching the back door he turns the knob and the door isn't locked. "Great!" He says to himself as he very slowly turns it until he can open the door without making any noise. Tiptoeing into the kitchen he can hear the two girls talking in the TV room. Not knowing exactly how he's going to handle the situation with Samantha, he knows he'll think of something. He's just glad that he'd thought enough to grab a piece of rope he found lying on the floor of the shed, and, of course, he has his knife he carries with him at all times, neatly stuck in his boot top.

Sweat was starting to run down his neck as he plants himself against the wall at the end of the kitchen.

As he starts to turn into the TV room, he steps on a pencil on the floor and it makes a crunch noise.

"What was that?" Samantha asks nervously turning around in her chair to look in the direction of the noise.

"I don't know!" Amanda says as she jumps up off the couch to see what it was. Frightened, she tells Samantha to stay put as she puts her finger to her lips to quiet her. Just as Amanda reaches the doorway Jacob rounds the corner and grabs her around the neck.

"Just be quiet and don't make a sound Amanda and you won't get hurt," Jacob says motioning for her to set back down on the couch.

"*Jacob!*" Samantha shouts. "*Don't hurt her. She did nothing to you and I know that it's me you are after. Just let her go and I'll go with you.*"

"I'll bet you will, Samantha," Jacob says as he takes his knife out of his pocket and holds it to Amanda's throat. "And as soon as we leave, Amanda will tell your *man* friend when he shows up just who has you, and he'll come looking for me, for us. *Not on your life!*" Jacob says as he takes the knife and in one split second slits Amanda's throat.

Blood is gushing out of Amanda's throat as Jacob releases her and she falls to the floor.

"*You son of a bitch!*" Samantha screams as she lunges towards Jacob.

"How could you do that to her and to Courtney? You will pay for this you bastard!" She says as she's beating on his chest. "You are mine again, Samantha," Jacob says as he grabs her fists to stop her from beating on his chest. "Courtney is no longer in our way and we can be together again, and it doesn't look as if Amanda is going to be a threat."

"Now, Samantha, just come with me and everything will be fine!" Jacob says as he starts to back through the kitchen, with his arm around Samantha's waist, dragging her as he goes.

"I am not going with you Jacob and you can't make me!" Samantha shouts as she tries to break free of him with her arms, and is kicking him in the shins. She then bites him on his arm.

"Ouch, you little shit!" Jacob screams. "You'd best behave yourself or else I will have to take greater measures to shut you up, and I don't believe that is what you want, is it, Samantha?"

"I will take any measures necessary to get away from you Jacob. And don't think for a minute that I can't do it!"

Knowing Samantha is still going to put up quite a fight, Jacob takes the rope out of his back pocket and tries to tie Samantha's hands behind her back to help stabilize her as not to do any more harm to him, and places his handkerchief over her mouth. He then tries to get her out of the apartment and into his SUV without anyone seeing them, and while Samantha is still struggling to get free.

Finally with both of them in the SUV Jacob starts the engine and pulls away from Amanda's apartment and heads back to the shed.

"Where in the hell are you Tyler and why weren't you right behind us when we left?" Samantha is asking herself as she struggles to try and free her hands while sitting in Jacob's SUV. "Oh Amanda!" She cries visualizing her lying there on the floor of her apartment.

Tyler's pulling up to Amanda's apartment applying his brakes and jumping out of his car. Not knowing what he is about to walk into, he knocks on her door. No one answers and he gets a little worried. He knows full well that the two girls left and came here straight from the library. "Amanda? Samantha?" He hollers. "Are the two of you in there?" Still no answer and he really is starting to worry. Backing up a few steps he lifts his right leg and kicks open the front door.

"Oh my God!" He shouts as he sees Amanda lying in the hallway in a pool of blood. He kneels down next to Amanda to take her pulse and there is none. He immediately looks for the nearest phone, which is on her desk and dials 911. He explains the situation and hangs up. "Now where is Samantha?" He asks himself out loud.

"*Damn it, you son of a bitch*!" He says as he slams his fist on the desk. "*You were following her and* now *you have her. I will not stop till I find you and you had better not hurt Sam!*"

Thinking of what to do till the police and ambulance arrive he knows he must call George.

"George, this is Tyler".

"Hello, Tyler what's going on? You sound a little anxious, is anything wrong?"

"That son of a bitch has killed Amanda and now he has Sam!" Tyler screams.

"*No!*" George exclaims. "I knew he was trouble and I had this feeling he was right behind the two of you all along. "Damn it, Tyler! How far ahead of you do you think Jacob is?"

"Only about ten minutes, George," Tyler explains. "I got stopped in the library and was detained. My God, George, I'm worried about Samantha! I'm in love with her, you know!" He cries. "Jacob must have been right outside the library waiting on us and took advantage of the situation when the two girls came out alone!"

"Tyler, I'm on my way. Don't do anything stupid. When the police arrive give them the necessary information and they can help you look for Samantha." George explains.

"But George what can you do? I've already got myself out on a limb and what do you think you can do?"

"Probably nothing, but Samantha is my employee and I couldn't live with myself if something should happen to her," George exclaims. "I'll be there just as soon as I can. I'll catch up with you at the motel."

"Drive carefully, George," Tyler says as he hears the sirens screaming as they come down the street. "The police and ambulance are here now. I'll see you when you get here."

Before hanging up the phone, Tyler gives George his cell phone number and then opens the door for the police and ambulance attendants.

"I'm Lieutenant Sanders," the policeman states. "What's happened here?"

Tyler explains the situation to the lieutenant as the ambulance attendants are checking on Amanda.

"Lieutenant Sanders," the attendant says. "This young lady is dead."

"I'm sorry, Mr. Worth," Lieutenant Sanders says. "Do you have any idea where we may start looking for this character, Jacob?"

"No, Lieutenant, actually I don't," Tyler says as he rubs his eyes with his left thumb and fingers. "But someone at the university might be able to help us. We can go back to the library and talk to Christina, the head librarian. We'll have to let her know about Amanda anyway, and she'll be able to help us get in touch with Amanda's family."

"You've been through enough for one day Mr. Worth, why don't you go back to your motel and we'll stay in touch with you," the lieutenant states. "I can go over to the library and talk to her."

"No way!" Tyler exclaims. "I want to find Sam as soon as possible, before he has a chance to hurt her. I'm staying with you."

"Fine," the lieutenant says. "But you are going to have to let us do our job and keep your distance. We don't want another casualty on our hands."

"Sure, but let's get going shall we?" Tyler asks. "That son of a bitch has a head start on us and we have to find him before he harms Sam."

"We'll take this young lady," the ambulance attendant states. "We'll take her to the hospital morgue until the next of kin can be notified and arrangements can be made as to where to take her body."

"Thanks," the lieutenant says. "Mr. Worth, let's not waste any more time here. We need to get to the university library now."

Tyler takes one last look at Amanda, shakes his head and heads for the front door.

Tyler fills Lieutenant Sanders in on the situation as best he can as they head for the library. Once at the university they take the front steps two at a time to get to the library and they spot Christina behind the counter waiting on a customer.

"Christina?" Tyler asks anxiously. "May we speak to you privately please?"

"Yes, of course," Christina says wondering why he's returned so quickly after just leaving a short time ago. "Thank you miss, I hope I've been of help to you and enjoy your book." She exclaims to the customer.

"Please come with me," Christina says motioning to the two men. "We can go into my office."

"Has something happened?"

"Yes, Christina," Tyler states. "I'm afraid we have some bad news. I went to Amanda's apartment right after leaving here, but I'm afraid I didn't arrive in time. Jacob must have been following Samantha and me from Palmetto. He's killed Amanda and has kidnapped Samantha."

"*Oh, my God!*" Christina shouts as she breaks down. "Not Amanda! Why would he want to harm her?"

Tyler grabs Christina's arm and helps her to a chair. "I'm sorry Christina to have to break such bad news to you, but I'm afraid we need your help. We need to know anything and everything you can tell us about Jacob while he was a student here. He's taken Samantha somewhere and we need to get to them fast, before he does something to her also."

Crying, Christina realizes that she must pull herself together and help these gentlemen before something else tragic happens. "Please just give me a minute to pull myself together and I'll do the best I can to help you."

"That's okay," Tyler says.

Gathering her thoughts, Christina grabs the phone and calls student records to see what information she can get from them.

"Student Records," the voice on the other end of the line answers. "May I help you?"

"Yes, this is Christina from the student library" she says. "I'm afraid I need some information on a former student ASAP. I have a Lieutenant Sanders in my office that has some questions. I'm going to put him on the phone now."

"Miss, I'm Lieutenant Sanders from downtown," Lieutenant Sanders states.

After the lieutenant is satisfied he has enough information from student records he thanks the girl on the other end of the line, hangs up, and looks at Tyler. "I don't have much, but a little is better than nothing. I did find out he had a part-time job while attending here his senior year. She was able to give me the name of the maintenance supervisor. Let's get moving and find this guy. Maybe he can enlighten us a little, on Jacob's comings and goings when he worked for him. I have an idea he didn't go far with Samantha. He knows you aren't far behind him and he's had to find a place to take her fast. My guess is, he never left the university. He spent four years here and I'm sure he knows his way around pretty well."

It was getting late in the day and they needed to get to moving before the head maintenance man left for the day, if it wasn't already too late. Tyler and Lieutenant Sanders leave the library and head for the maintenance shop as fast as they can. Upon their arrival, there is only one person left in the shop and he tells them the head honcho, Bob Stevens, left early that day for an appointment, and wouldn't be back till his regular shift in the morning.

"Son," Lieutenant Sanders says. "Do you have a few minutes that I may ask you a few questions regarding a former employee?"

"I'm sorry sir, but I was just hired for summer help. I'm afraid I wouldn't be of any help to you," the young man says.

"I'm sorry too," states the lieutenant. "Do you have the phone number of Bob Stevens?"

"No, I'm sorry I don't," the young man says. "If I'm not going to be at work, I call the university personnel office and they take it from there to report it to my supervisor."

"Thank you," the lieutenant says. "Tyler lets go, we're wasting our time here. Thank you very much for your time." He says as he tips his hat to the young man.

"Tyler, I'm sure by the time we'd get back to the personnel office they'll be closed also. We just barely got under the wire when we called them earlier. I'm going to call into headquarters and have them look up this Bob Steven's number and hopefully we can get a hold of him at home."

"Fine." Tyler says. "I only hope he's home. I'm really worried about Sam, lieutenant."

"I'm sure you are Tyler" the lieutenant says. "Why don't I run you by the motel and you can wait on George?"

"No way, Lieutenant. I'm staying right here with you. When George gets here he has my cell phone number and he'll get a hold of me. I'm not waiting in any motel room when he's out there with Sam."

"Okay, I was only trying to help you. You look like hell, if you don't mind me saying so. You've already been through a lot today and it's about to get longer."

"I can handle it Lieutenant. I just want to find Samantha."

The lieutenant proceeds to call into headquarters to find Bob Stevens' phone number. The receptionist answering the call enters the information from the lieutenant into the computer and is waiting for it to come up on the screen. It's only moments and she's on the line. "Lieutenant, I think I have what you want. This Mr. Stevens lives close to the university. Where are you right now?"

The lieutenant tells her their location and she gives them directions from where they are currently. Of course the lieutenant is pretty sure where the address is himself and is starting the police car and is already on his way.

"I only hope he's home." Tyler exclaims. "I'd really like to be able to search this evening instead of waiting till later or even in the morning."

"Me too." states the lieutenant. "The longer we are behind what this Jacob is up to, the harder it is going to be to find them. Even if he isn't home yet, we can still ride around and search the university area. You said you thought you have a pretty good description of his SUV from the incidents you described to me earlier."

"Yes, I do, but there must be a ton of black SUV's around, Lieutenant," Tyler says.

The lieutenant is dialing Mr. Steven's number as they speak. The phone is ringing and he gets an answer, but a lady answers.

"Hello," the voice answers.

"Is this Mrs. Stevens?" The lieutenant asks. "I'm police Lieutenant Sanders from the down town headquarters. Is your husband at home?"

"No, I'm sorry he isn't," she says. "Is there something wrong? Is my husband okay?"

"Yes, Mrs. Stevens," your husband is just fine. I want to talk to him about a former employee of his at the university. Do you have any idea about when he will be home? It's very important that I speak with him as soon as possible."

"He left work early today for an appointment and then he is going over to a buddy's house to play cards tonight. I won't see him until much later tonight."

"Damn!" The lieutenant whispers under his breathe. "Could you give me the number of his buddy, Mrs. Stevens? I hate to be such a pest but I must talk with him."

"No problem," she says. "Just give me a moment to look it up in my address book."

"Lieutenant?" Tyler asks, getting a little impatient. "What is going on here?"

"Mr. Stevens isn't home yet and in fact, he isn't coming straight home. He's going to play cards at a buddy's house and won't be home till much later. I'm waiting now for the missus to get the phone number of the buddy for me."

"*Well holy shit!*" Tyler exclaims. "We're just wasting time lieutenant!"

"Now just calm down, Tyler. We're doing the best we can here." Mrs. Stevens comes back on the line and gives the lieutenant the phone number and address. "I don't believe they usually start playing till around 6:30. Bob was planning on stopping to grab something to eat before going over to play cards."

"Thank you Mrs. Stevens," the lieutenant says. "You've been a great help." He hangs up the phone and looks at Tyler.

"How about if the two of us grab something to eat and then check out this card game?" The lieutenant asks Tyler. "You look as if you could use something."

"*Hell no*!" Tyler shrieks. "Lieutenant, I'm afraid for Samantha. Can we either go over to this guys house or give him a call and tell him to have Mr. Stevens call us as soon as he arrives.

"Fine," the lieutenant says. He dials the number and the phone rings once and is picked up. "This is Lieutenant Sanders sir. I'm looking for Bob Stevens and I understand from his wife that he is due there around 6:30. It's imperative that I speak with him as soon as possible. Could you have him call this number as soon as he arrives?"

"Sure. Is there anything wrong?" The man asks.

"Nothing that concerns Mr. Stevens. We just want some information from him. I'm not at liberty to expand on this, as I'm sure you'll understand, but would appreciate it if you could honor our request and have him call."

"I'm sorry, I will have him call just as soon as he gets here," the gentleman says.

"Thank you very much for your time," the lieutenant says and hangs up.

"Tyler whether you are hungry or not I am, and I think we should grab a bite, regroup and then see what we can do."

"Okay, if you're hungry then let's go, but I couldn't eat if I wanted to. I just want to find Sam."

Chapter Fifteen

Jacob arrived safely at the shed with Samantha. However it wasn't easy. She put up quite a fight and even tried to break out a side window with her feet. Once at the shed Jacob made sure no one was around before attempting to get her inside. He knew she would put up another fight and try to get loose.

"Samantha, you are going to have to calm down and cooperate with me. I don't want to have to hurt you. But if I have to I will." Jacob says rather calmly to her. "I want you to walk in there with me and in an orderly fashion. If you try to scream no one will hear you with that rag in your mouth, so don't waste your time. Also kicking me isn't going to get you anywhere, so just remain calm okay?"

"You are out of your mind you son of a bitch." Samantha says to herself. "If you think for one minute I'm not going to give you a fight."

Jacob tries to open the door to the shed with Samantha kicking and trying to scream, but with the rag in her mouth nothing is coming out. "Damn!" She says to herself.

"Samantha, it will be much easier for you if you just cooperate," Jacob says as he tightens his hand around her arm. I'm not going to harm you, but if you continue to act up I can guarantee that you will not like the results."

Entering the shed Jacob closes the door. As he does so, he glances around to see if anyone has heard Samantha's disturbance or has seen them pull up. He'd pulled around to the back so the SUV wouldn't be seen. It was very deserted behind the shed and there would be no way anyone would see it unless the maintenance supervisor would come snooping around, and he doubted that would happen considering the time of day it is. They would have been off work for a while now. Also the SUV is black and once it gets dark no one will be able to spot it anyway. There also were no visible lights around the old shed.

Jacob has already released the hold he has on Samantha's arm and has given her a little shove inside. She was trying to get her balance and bearings on just where Jacob had brought her when she looks around and sees that it is an old athletic storage shed. The smell is atrocious and there is old used football equipment stacked everywhere. The room smells like an old, sweaty boy's locker room. She stumbles a little and notices there is a blanket spread out on the floor. Looking around she doesn't see any lights. The sun will be setting in a few hours and things will get a little spooky. She isn't surprised that this is where Jacob brought her. He needed to get her somewhere fast, before Tyler figured out what had happened and could get a description out on the SUV to the police. She knew that Jacob had worked some maintenance while in attendance here at the university, but had no idea it was in the athletic department.

Taking another assessment of her surroundings, Samantha notices the blanket again and a few other things that you wouldn't normally find in an equipment storage shed. "Jacob, is this where you and Courtney would meet secretly?" She asks turning to look at him as he's removing the gag from her mouth again.

"Boy it didn't take you long to figure that one out did it?" Jacob answers sarcastically. "You were always quick on the draw weren't you? That must be why you make such a good investigative reporter," he says as he stretches his arm over the stack of old football helmets to move the drab white curtain at the small window aside, to make another check outside to make sure no one was coming.

"Getting a little nervous are we Jacob?" Samantha asks watching him peak out the window.

"No, why do you ask that?" He asks as he lets the curtain fall back into place.

"You keep looking outside to see if anyone is coming, that's why," she says. "Don't worry, Tyler will be here in no time. He also is an excellent investigative reporter and he'll find me and then you are history!" She says shouting at him and wiping her hand over her forehead. It is really stuffy and warm in the shed. After all it is the middle of the summer in South Carolina.

"So that is the name of *your friend* that you've been hanging around with for the past several weeks," Jacob says as he steps closer to Samantha. "I've been following the two of you rather closely for some time now. I followed the two of you pretty much the whole Fourth of July weekend. It looked to me like it was more than just a working relationship. The two of you spent the night out on the boat didn't you?" He asks getting a little nervous.

"It's none of your business what my relationship with Tyler is!" Samantha exclaims moving a step back away from him and noticing at the same time that he's perspiring profusely and getting more nervous. She's sure the conversation about Tyler is getting his dander up, and knowing now what he is capable of is scaring her.

"Well as a matter of fact I no longer care what your relationship with him is because you are no longer his, you are mine!" He says with fire in his eyes that Samantha has never seen before. "I should never have broken it off with you in the first place. If it hadn't been for Courtney finding out about the two of us I wouldn't have. But she had to go and spoil it all. So I broke it off with you, but that didn't satisfy her. She was a friend of yours and she couldn't handle it, so she tried to break it off with me. Well she paid for that didn't she?"

"*Jacob you are sick!*" Samantha shouts. "How could you do that to Courtney? You will not get away with it. Tyler will leave no stones unturned. He *will* find me Jacob!"

Jacob grabs her around the neck and pulls her face to his. "And if he doesn't?" He asks. "What then, Samantha? I'll tell you what then! I'm taking you far away from here and no one will find us. As soon as the heat is off, we're out of here!" He says as he plants a hard kiss on her lips.

Samantha tries to pull away but can't. It makes her nauseous to have his lips on hers or for him to be anywhere near her. As he releases his lips from hers she wipes her mouth off with the back of her hand and spits. "Get away from me Jacob! And if you touch me again I'll start screaming and I won't stop until someone hears me or I lose my voice!"

"Oh aren't we the heroic one. I can silence you in no time, so I suggest you calm down and make yourself comfortable. We are going to be here for a while," he says as he points toward the blanket he'd put on the floor earlier.

"I'm hungry Jacob," Samantha says. "Did you even think to bring anything to eat?" She was thinking that she hadn't seen anything in the SUV, and she certainly didn't see any food here in the shed. If he'd have to go out she might be able to make a break for it and get help while it is still daylight.

"No, I didn't!" He chuckles. "How did I know the idiot was going to let you and Amanda out of his sight and make it so easy for me? If I'd known, you better believe I'd have brought food so I wouldn't have to leave your side. Not much of a bodyguard is he? I'll go get something for you, what would you like?"

"A hamburger would be just fine," Samantha says. "I don't want to eat much because it's too hot. This place stinks and makes me ill!"

"Well I'm sorry, Samantha, but convenience wasn't what I had in mind at the time," he said sarcastically as he heads towards her again. "Just so you won't do anything stupid while I'm gone," he says as he puts the rag in her mouth again so she won't be screaming at the top of her lungs while he's gone.

As Jacob opens the door she lunges at him to try to get out but at no avail. He immediately puts his leg in front of her and shoves her back into a stack of the old equipment. "Nice try Samantha," he says as he shuts the door in disgust. "Now do you want something to eat or not? I can just as easily stay here."

Trying to pick herself up off the equipment isn't easy with her hands tied behind her back and the rag stuffed in her mouth made her breathing a little uneasy. As a matter of fact it was making her gag and she's attempting to cough. She's beginning to get a little more frightened and wondering just what he is capable of if he doesn't mind hurting her.

The look in her eyes tells Jacob that she is a little frightened after being shoved. "Don't try that again Samantha!" He exclaims as he opens the door.

"I'll be back shortly, and in the meantime, I suggest that you calm yourself down. I do mean business," he says as he goes out and locks the door behind him.

Samantha hears him put the key in the door to lock it. "I have to find my way out of here before he returns," she says to herself as she's frantically looking around for options and hears him leaving in the SUV. She notices her back hurts a little after being shoved in the equipment. "Surely I can make it out this window if I can climb up there and somehow break it," she says to herself. But climbing the stack isn't that easy. As she tries to pull herself up onto the top of the equipment she causes the stack to come tumbling down around her, she looses her footing and falls on her tailbone. "Ouch!" She says as she's trying to regain her balance and stand back up. Standing back up she is trying to kick the equipment out of the way when she realizes that without it stacked she will not be able to use her feet to kick the glass out and she can use no other part of her body with her arms tied behind her back. Looking around she becomes very frustrated and sees no other alternatives to getting out any time soon. "Damn," she says to herself and tears weld up in her eyes. ""Where are you Tyler?" She cries as the tears stream down her face.

Chapter Sixteen

Tyler and Lieutenant Sanders stop at the nearest local diner to eat. "How's this?" The lieutenant says to Tyler? "These are the best places to eat. I get tired of the fast food places."

"Fine!" Tyler grumbles. He was hoping he'd stop at a fast food place though. This is going to take up too much time. "Doesn't he know time is of the essence?" He says to himself. Looking at his watch he is getting even more concerned about Sam. He knows that she is probably scared out of her mind. "Hang in there, Sam," he says out loud not knowing the lieutenant hears him.

"What?" The lieutenant asks as the waitress approaches to take their order.

"Nothing." says Tyler.

The lieutenant places his order, but Tyler only orders an iced tea. He's in no mood to eat. It isn't long before the food arrives but for Tyler it seems like an eternity. "You know Tyler," the lieutenant reminds him as he takes a bite of his hamburger. "You aren't doing yourself or Samantha any good. She's going to need you so you'd best try to remain calm and you'd better get something in your stomach. It's going to be a long night."

As Tyler's patience is wearing thin, his cell phone in his pocket rings. "Hello," he says. "Good to hear from you George."

"I'm at the motel Tyler. Have you had any luck finding Samantha?"

"No," Tyler says as he moves his chair back to get up and heads outside for better reception and to put some distance between he and the lieutenant so he can talk to George without the lieutenant hearing. He nods to the lieutenant as he leaves.

Once outside the reception is better. "George, I am getting very frustrated."

"Where are you now? I'll meet you there."

"No, George, stay put. We'll come pick you up. The lieutenant was hungry and said we needed to take a break. Damn it, George. He's wasting time. We need to find Sam before something happens to her. I can't even begin to eat anything."

"Come by and pick me up as soon as he's through. I've been in contact with our police department and they have already made contact with the department here. They are on it now and have a clearer picture of what's going on."

"Great!" Tyler exclaims. "Maybe they can knock some sense into this lieutenant's head and we can get moving on this. It shouldn't take long here and we should hear from the head maintenance man from the university soon. I'm hoping he can shed some light on this and maybe be able to give us some insights on Jacob. I'll see you soon." Tyler says and pushes the button on his cell phone to disconnect George.

As Tyler enters the diner he sees the lieutenant is disconnecting his cell phone also. He hurries over to see if it was Mr. Stevens. "Was that the maintenance man from the university?" Tyler asks.

"Yes, it was." Lieutenant Sanders answers. "He really couldn't give me too much info other than Jacob did work during his senior year at the university. He didn't directly work with him because he was assigned to other maintenance men under him and unfortunately some of them were on vacation also. But he'll get with them the first thing in the morning and have them on the look out at the university and also ask them if they ever saw anything peculiar about Jacob. It seems he'd met Courtney when she'd meet Jacob after work on occasion and thought she was a very sweet young lady. He'd heard what had happened to her and just couldn't believe it when I told him that we were looking for Jacob. Of course I couldn't give him too many of the particulars and he understood that."

"Well at least that's a start," Tyler says seeing that the lieutenant has just about finished his food. "That was George. I told him as soon as you were finished here we'd pick him up at the motel."

"Fine," the lieutenant says putting his napkin in his plate and standing up. "I'm through here. Just let me take care of this tab and I'm ready to go. You know you really should have eaten something."

"I know. Can we just go now? I'm very anxious to find her and I feel the longer we wait, the less our chances of finding her are," Tyler says as he gets his billfold out to pay for his iced tea.

It only takes about fifteen minutes to get to the motel and pick up George. Tyler takes care of the formalities of introducing George to Lieutenant Sanders.

"Nice to meet you lieutenant," George says. "Is Tyler here giving you any trouble?"

"No, not really," the lieutenant says. "I know he's concerned about Samantha."

"Well if you don't mind can we go by your office lieutenant?" George asks. "Our department has been in contact with yours and I'd like to see what, if anything, new they have for us."

"I've been keeping in touch with them and they haven't had any luck yet either, but if you'd like, we can touch base with them before we canvas the university from end to end," Lieutenant Sanders says.

All three men enter headquarters and go straight to the captain's office. His door is open and Lieutenant Sanders is used to going right on in and urges the others to follow.

"Good evening Captain Holmes." the lieutenant says. "This is George Chambliss and Tyler Worth from Palmetto."

"Hello, gentlemen." Captain Holmes says. "I'm sorry to say that none of my men have had any luck. I have an all points bulletin out on this guy and his vehicle."

"Captain," Lieutenant Sanders says." If you don't mind, I'd like to take these two men with me and go over the university with a fine tooth comb. Jacob was here for four years and worked maintenance his senior year. He surely knows this university like the back of his hand. Also, Tyler here definitely knows what he looks like as well as Samantha and he knows the SUV. And George here is Samantha's boss. If I take one, I need to take both of them."

"You know that isn't office policy Lieutenant," the captain states. "No! I'll have the mayor on my back so fast if he finds out, we'll both be out of here and quite frankly I like my job and I need it."

"It is either take them with me so I can keep an eye on them, or else they'll be out there on their own looking for Samantha and our suspect."

"Lieutenant, I can see trouble written all over this, but just this once I'll let the three of you go. If you don't follow the lieutenant's instructions," the captain says pointing his finger at both George and Tyler, you are out and I mean it. Do both of you understand me?"

"Yes, Sir," Tyler says. "Thank you so much. All I want is to find Samantha."

"Now get out of here and find that girl, Lieutenant," Captain Holmes says. " I want her alive."

Chapter Seventeen

When Jacob returns with the food, it's dark and he feels safe driving behind the shed to hide his SUV. "It will really be hard to spot this black SUV now," he laughs to himself. "That is if they even search the university. They may think I'm long gone with Samantha and aren't even looking here. At least that is what I'm hoping."

He balances the bag of food and soft drinks he picked up at McDonald's between his arm and hip and tries to insert the key into the keyhole in the dark. He doesn't hit the keyhole the first try and feels around with his fingers to find the hole. "Samantha, why don't you come and open the door?" He whispers loudly, but realizes she wouldn't be cooperative. He knows she's heard him drive up. "She isn't making this whole situation easy on herself," he grunts as he finds the keyhole with his finger and tries to reinsert the key. This time he succeeds and turns the doorknob to open the door.

Once inside he closes the door and immediately sees the mess of equipment on the floor and remembers he left her hands tied so she couldn't let him in.

"Have a good time while I was gone, Samantha?" He laughs seeing her sitting on the blanket on the floor with her hands tied behind her back and the gag in her mouth. It's hard to see now, because the only light they have, is from a light outside the building that only illuminates the room just enough to see. Jacob made sure of that when he'd bring Courtney here and they wanted the privacy. She really doesn't look very comfortable and the look on her face could kill. "If I untie your hands and take your gag out, will you promise not to try to escape again or scream?"

Samantha nods her head yes as Jacob leans down to untie her hands and remove the rag from her mouth. She really isn't at all hungry, but guesses she'd better eat something to keep up her strength in case she does get lucky enough to escape. Lifting herself up off the blanket, she can feel the pain in her butt from her not- so- soft landing while attempting to climb the equipment and break the window. She walks over to the McDonald's bag to see what Jacob's brought to eat. She takes out a cheeseburger and fries and gets herself a drink out of the carry tray all the while attempting to look out the window to see if she can see anyone outside.

She then starts to move towards the blanket and notices Jacob is headed there also. "There is no way in hell that I'm sitting with him on that blanket," she says to herself as she moves to a place on the other side of the room, where she sits down on the bare floor and leans up against another stack of equipment to eat.

"What's the matter, Samantha, you afraid of me?" He asks as he sits down on the blanket and sets his drink down beside him.

"Funny, Jacob," Samantha says. "You won't have me here long, I can guarantee it. He will find me soon."

"What makes you so sure, Samantha? I use to come here all the time with Courtney and there was never anyone around. This old equipment hasn't been touched in years. Football practice doesn't start for another month and they won't use this old stuff anyway. We will be safe here for a long time. Once they realize they can't find you and I feel the heat is off, I'll be able to take you out of the country," Jacob says as he takes another bite of his fries and sets his drink back down on the blanket.

"I'm going nowhere with you, you jerk," she exclaims wadding her cheeseburger wrapper up and tossing it at him. "So just get that idea out of your head."

Samantha finishes her fries and realizes she has eaten more than she thought she could. Getting up off the floor she starts over to the other side of the room to put the remainder of her paper in the empty sack and as she does Jacob grabs her hand and pulls her down on the blanket beside him, before she knows what is happening.

"Don't touch me, Jacob," Samantha screams as she tries to pull free of him by using her other hand to pry his hand that is now around her arm.

"Shut up you bitch!" Jacob exclaims. "Sit down here and behave yourself or I will have to tie you back up and put that gag back in your mouth. I'd really prefer not to have to do that because I have other things in mind for you."

"Oh, no, you don't," Samantha screams again, this time kicking him in the stomach.

Jacob grabs her leg just as she kicks him in the stomach and she falls into his lap. "Now I have you right where I wanted you the minute I got you here, Samantha." He rolls her over on her back and climbs on top of her with his legs straddling her. She tries to work her arms loose but he's got them pinned down on the blanket up over her head. "You remember, just as I do, the way we use to make love," he says as he leans down and tries to kiss her.

But Samantha brings her knee up and rams it into his groin area and he falls forward. "Get off me, Jacob!" Samantha screams as he falls forward. She successfully gets up and runs for the door while Jacob is picking himself up off the floor. Just as he rolls over he catches Samantha's foot and she falls to the floor hitting her head on one of the helmets and knocks her out.

Jacob decides to let her come to on her own. Seeing she isn't going to cooperate and keep quiet, he drags her over to the blanket and reties her hands behind her back and puts the gag in her mouth. "Won't she be surprised when she wakes up," he says out loud while placing the gag in her mouth. "Maybe now she'll know I mean business." It was already after nine and he's exhausted. Samantha will be out for a while so he decides to get some sleep, being reasonably sure that they are safe for now.

Chapter Eighteen

Lieutenant Sanders, George and Tyler search the university campus for over three hours and haven't seen even a glimpse of a black SUV. "I don't know about you two, but I've had it for one day. We don't even know if Jacob has Samantha on campus. The two of them could be long gone by now. I'm going to take the two of you back to the motel and we can start out again at daybreak."

"Maybe you're right," George yawns running his fingers through his hair. "Tyler why don't we get some rest? You've had a pretty rough day and you look like hell. I'm sure Jacob won't harm Samantha if she cooperates with him."

"How can you be so sure George? Look what he's done to Courtney and now Amanda. I can't believe for one second that Sam is safe with him. I have to keep looking for her George. Lieutenant, remember my car is at Amanda's. Will you take me back there to get it and I think I'll keep looking for a while longer?"

"No, Tyler!" George exclaims. "Lieutenant, take us to the motel. Tyler can leave his car at Amanda's. You can pick us up in the morning, we can get his car then and bring it back to the motel. But right now, I'm not letting him out of my sight."

"George, please!" Shouts Tyler frantically. "I can't stand the thought of that murderer out there with Samantha all night."

"Tyler there isn't much we can do about that now. All three of us have to have our rest."

"I know it's not easy for you, but we'll start out fresh in the morning. The night shift will continue to search for the SUV. Maybe they will get lucky. But in the mean time I'm taking you back to the motel."

"Thanks for everything lieutenant," George says as they arrive back at the motel. "What time will you be back for us in the morning?"

"I'll be here by seven," the lieutenant says. "Now the two of you get some rest and I'll see you in the morning. Hang in there Tyler. We have a good force here and I'm sure something will turn up."

Once the lieutenant leaves, Tyler starts for his room retrieving his key from his pocket. "George, did you have time to get a room when you got here?"

"No, I didn't," George says yawning again.

"Come on then, you can room with me," Tyler says motioning George towards the room with his arm. Tyler enters the room and plops down on the edge of the king sized bed. Looking up at George his eyes start to tear up. "George what am I going to do?" He asks as he starts to cry like a baby. "I'm really worried about her."

George walks over and sits on the bed next to Tyler. "I know you are Tyler. We'll just have to pray and keep our heads up. We'll find her Tyler I know we will. She's a very strong girl and can take care of herself. I only wish right now, that I wouldn't have let the two of you come here anyway. If we'd left this job to the authorities like we should have, this wouldn't have happened. We've lost another young lady and we can't find Samantha. Now let's get some sleep." George gets up off of the bed and starts loosening his tie.

"I know you're worried too George," Tyler says. "I'm sorry."

"She's a pretty special girl. I've known her a long time," George says as he continues to undress. "If you don't mind I think I'll take a shower."

"No, go ahead, George," Tyler says getting the remote control to turn on the TV. Just as the TV comes on Tyler hears the newscaster talking about Amanda's murder. He turns the volume up and listens to what he has to say. They had a camera at the scene and were showing the paramedics wheeling Amanda out on the stretcher, her body covered with a white sheet. "Oh God," Tyler says. "Please don't let him do this to, Sam."

When George comes out of the bathroom a few minutes later he finds Tyler lying on the bed clothes and all, sound asleep with the TV remote control still in his hand. "Poor guy." George says to himself out loud. "I hope nothing happens to her. This guy will be devastated." George takes the TV remote control out of Tyler's hand, pushes the button and turns around to get into his bed. As he does so, it hits him that he promised Samantha's parents he'd give them a call a soon as he could and let them know if they needed to make the trip to the university to help find their daughter. He'd assured them to stay put, that it wouldn't do them any good to come that far, but he'd keep in touch with them.

Marty, Samantha's mother, is watching the news when the phone rings.

She practically runs to the phone that's on a side table on the other side of the room. At the same time her husband Curtis comes around the corner from the kitchen to grab the phone. The two of them glance at each other with fear in their eyes. Not hearing from George sooner than this, if this indeed is him, isn't encouraging news. "Just stay calm." Curtis says as he picks up the receiver, covers it with his hand and makes a calming motion with his other hand. "Hello, George," Curtis says. "Have you found Samantha, and is she okay?"

"No, I'm sorry to say we haven't. We've been combing the university area all afternoon and evening and have come up empty. We are hoping the night shift has better luck, if they indeed are still in the area. I have a feeling they are still here, knowing that we would have an APB out on the SUV and it would be hard to escape.

Curtis is shaking his head no to Marty, letting her know that they haven't had any luck as yet. "How's Tyler?" He asks as Marty sits down on the sofa and starts to sob uncontrollably.

"We just arrived back here at the motel. He's emotionally spent and just fell asleep on top of the bed in his clothes. That's when I realized I hadn't touched base with you. I sincerely apologize. We are doing everything here that we can. I'll be lucky to keep Tyler in here till morning. He is so worried about Samantha, as well am I," he says as he runs his fingers through his hair and yawns.

"Marty and I will drive there first thing in the morning," he says to George. "I can't stand it here any longer. We may not be of much help, but Marty can't stand this any longer either."

"Fine," George says knowing that's exactly what he would do if it were his daughter. "I can't ask you to stay there any longer. But when you arrive you will have to stay here at the motel. I can't have you traipsing all over this town and university not knowing what you are doing, do you understand?"

Curtis told George they would abide by his wishes and George gave him the address and phone number to the motel and hung up. George walked over to Tyler's side of the bed, notices he's out like a light and covers him up with a blanket he found on the upper shelf in the motel closet. He then undresses and falls into bed.

Chapter Nineteen

The sun is shining brightly through the tiny window as Samantha awakens. It doesn't take her long to realize that her hands are tied and the gag is back in her mouth. She squirms to see how tight her hands are tied and accidentally rubs up against Jacob who is sleeping right beside her. "Oh God!" She whispers, realizing how close he's slept next to her. She wastes no time moving away before she awakens him. "How can I get myself out of here? It's not likely they are going to find me for quite some time." As she moves away she notices that his keys are lying next to him as if they'd fallen out of his pocket while he was sleeping. She sees that he isn't stirring and eases her way over closer to him, turns herself around with her feet and tries to locate the keys with her hands. "Yes!" She screams in a whisper as she feels the keys and manages to pick them up with her fingers. At the same time she hears Jacob stirring and must find a place to hide the keys before he does wake up and finds them in her hand. She moves over to the equipment closest to her and manages to put the keys into one of the helmets and repositions it so Jacob can't see the keys in it. "He won't even notice this helmet is moved," she says to herself as she sees that there is absolutely no organization to them at all. Whoever stacked them just piled them on, in no mannerly fashion whatsoever. Samantha then moves back over onto the blanket as Jacob rolls over and awakens.

"Good morning, my love," Jacob says as he sets up on the blanket and reaches over and removes the gag from her mouth.

"What's good about it?" Samantha asks sarcastically.

"Now, now. Don't be sarcastic. Did you sleep well last night?" He asks as he rubs the side of his hand along her right cheek.

Samantha can only manage to twist her head the other direction to ward off his hand. It gives her chills down her spine knowing he's touching her.

"Please don't be that way," he says moving closer to her and realizes touching her that he wants her even more now. He doesn't stop there. He's close enough that he places his hand gently around her neck and pulls her to him so he can kiss her.

"*No!*" She exclaims as she uses her feet to move herself away from him and backs into the row of equipment behind her. "Please Jacob, No!" She screams as she realizes she can't move any further away from him and tries to ward him off with her feet.

Jacob however cannot resist. He wants her and he is going to have her, *now*. "Samantha, I remember when you used to enjoy making love to me," he says as he again moves closer to her. "I even remember the things that heightened your desire the most." He smiles as he pushes her feet away from him so he can wedge closer.

Samantha knows deep down that he isn't going to give in. She can see it in his eyes. "When did this all go wrong?" She asks herself. "And what went wrong with him?" She feels a sickness in her stomach that she's never felt before and knows what is going to happen next and isn't sure she has the capabilities of stopping it. Jacob's trying to lie her down, but she's determined not to make this easy for him. She will fight him all the way. If he does get his way with her, she'll make sure it isn't a pleasant one.

"Please, don't fight me on this," Jacob says as he's on his knees and manages to lay her down, but not before she gets her right foot into his chin. "Damn you, Samantha." Determination takes over as he pins her shoulders down and puts his right leg over her and straddles her at her waist. She's wriggling all the while and tries to kick him off but to no avail.

"*Jacob, please stop, I'm begging you*!" She cries as he moves his hands gently down her top. Her arms are killing her with her hands tied behind her back and she is left with no defenses whatsoever. Tears start to roll down her cheeks and he takes both his thumbs to dry them. "Oh God, please help me," she says as she's erratically moving her head back and forth.

"Samantha, I will not hurt you," he says as he manages to pull up her top and bra as she continually tries to resist him. Her breasts are as soft as he remembers. "I wish you would relax and enjoy this as much as I'm going to, Samantha."

Chapter Twenty

Tyler wakes up with a start and sees that the sun is just coming up. Looking over into the king-sized bed he sees that George is sleeping soundly. He has to get out of here and find Sam. Looking at his watch, he can't believe that he could have slept at all. She was out there with that monster and hard telling what he's done to her. Jumping out of bed he retrieves a change of clothes and quietly as he can tiptoes into the bathroom. He has to get out of here before George wakes up. He'd start looking for her by himself. "When George wakes up he can call me on my cell phone and join me, but right now I'm out of here," he says as he creeps out of the bathroom, picks his keys up off the side table and exits the room, hopefully not awaking George. Once outside he realizes his car is still at Amanda's. "Damn it," he shouts, knowing he has to call a cab, so he runs to the lobby to find a pay phone rather than risking re-entering the motel room and awakening George.

The cab arrives faster than he expects and he tells the driver where to take him. Once at Amanda's, he pays the cab driver and jumps into his car and speeds away from the curb, towards the university, to start looking. He'd driven old beat up cars until he was out of college and now is making a decent wage where he could afford a newer one and he's really proud of it. It's a navy ninety-eight Mitsubishi convertible sports car. It still looks brand new because he treats it like it's his baby, and it is.

"Okay, Sam, I promise I will find you and that bastard isn't going to harm you," he says out loud and grabs still tighter on the steering wheel.

He spots a McDonald's and pulls through the drive up for a cup of coffee and realizes he hasn't eaten since early yesterday, with Samantha. He was too upset to eat anything and he's starving now, so he orders an Egg McMuffin with his coffee. He can eat in the car while driving around the university. He wonders if Jacob is letting Samantha eat and whether he's taking good care of her. *Dear God.* He hoped he hasn't done something stupid and he prayed she's still alive. He couldn't bare it if something should happen to her. He's only known her a short while, but he's never felt like this about anyone before. He thought he'd been in love before, but nothing like this. She's completely blown him off his feet.

Arriving at the university, Tyler notices that the employees are arriving for work. He pulls up to the curb in front of the administration building. He's only going to be there long enough to run in and get directions to the maintenance building, so he doesn't bother to find a parking space. The lady at the front desk gives him the directions and he's back out to his car in a flash. He wastes no time locating the building and notices a man unlocking the front door to the building as he parks his car.

"Sir." Tyler says as he approaches and the gentleman hears him and turns around as he's stepping inside. "Good morning. I'm sorry to bother you. My name is Tyler Worth. I'm in town working on the case of Courtney Britton. Are you familiar with the case? She was a student here at the university a few years back"

"Yes," the gentleman says as he shuts the door behind Tyler and approaches his desk. "I was sorry to read about what happened to her. I did know her, because she use to come around to see one of my student employees while he worked for me. I believe it was Jacob. Yeah, it was Jacob. Fine boy he was and a hard worker too. But what does this have to do with me?" He asks.

"We have reason to believe that he may have murdered Courtney and now he's kidnapped the young lady I work with," Tyler says aware that the man he's talking to is no spring chicken and his memory may not be the best. "We believe that he may be hiding her somewhere here on campus. We practically turned this campus upside down yesterday and last night looking for them, but had no luck. Is there anywhere you know of that he might be hiding her?"

"Oh sir I'm so sorry," the gentleman says as he takes his time card to punch himself in for the day. "Let me think a minute about the areas Jacob use to work in. I've had so many student workers since him, I need to refresh my memory."

"I'm sorry sir, but I'm sure you understand that time is of the essence here. We need to find Samantha before he harms her," Tyler says getting a little impatient.

"I believe Jacob was in charge of the buildings where the athletic equipment is kept.

He was quite a sports enthusiast, so I figured he'd take good care of the equipment. And a fine job he did too. He took pride in his work. I never had to get on him about how he did things," he says taking off his hat and scratching his head.

"Can you tell me where these buildings are located on campus?" Tyler asks getting even more frustrated. "I would really like to check them out again. Are there any tucked away sort of out of sight, where someone could go and no one would know they were there? The police and I checked every building we could think of yesterday."

"Let me see," he says. "Yes!" He exclaims as is a light bulb is going on in his head. "There is one small shed that houses some of our old outdated equipment that isn't used any more. No one even goes out to there, no need to. We really need to discard all that old stuff, but no one seems to ever have time," he says shaking his head. "Seems no one has time to do anything any more."

Getting very antsy, Tyler gets the directions from the gentleman, and thanks him as he's practically running out of the building. "You've been a great help sir, thank you. If there's anything else, I'll get in touch with you." And Tyler's gone before the man has a chance to give him the key to the building.

"Hey, you need the key," the gentleman says shouting at Tyler, but he's already in his car and driving away. "Well I hope everything turns out okay," the man says to himself. "She was a mighty fine young lady. Jacob what kind of trouble have you gotten yourself into?" He turns to his staff who are one by one checking in for their assignments for the day.

Chapter Twenty-One

George wakes up, rolls over and immediately notices that Tyler isn't in bed. "Tyler you up?" He asks and gets no answer. He doesn't hear anyone in the restroom. He looks at his watch and it registers past seven am. Sitting up on the side of the bed, he hoists himself up, walks a few feet to the restroom and knocks on the door. "Tyler, you in there?" He again gets no response. "Damn it, Tyler. Where have you gone?" He asks as he goes to the front door to look and see if he's outside.

It doesn't take him long to put two and two together to know that he's taken out on his own to find Samantha. He calls the department to let them know that Tyler's left on his own and to have Lieutenant Sanders pick him up ASAP. In the meantime he takes a quick shower while he's waiting. "Tyler what are you thinking?" George asks.

"If you do manage to find Samantha, how in the world do you think you can handle Jacob on your own? He has, no doubt, at least a knife."

"Good morning, Lieutenant." George says as he opens the car door to get in.

"How in the hell did Tyler get out of your sight, George?" The lieutenant asks taking a sip of his coffee and returning it to it's holder.

"I guess he was exceptionally quiet or else I was so exhausted, I didn't hear a thing."

"Well I must say, the captain was very annoyed when you called. Jacob is for sure armed and dangerous and Tyler is probably out there trying to play the hero and as far as I know he doesn't even have a weapon, does he?"

"No, I'm sure he doesn't. We don't allow our employees to carry them, but they don't usually get this involved in cases either. They are suppose to report them, not solve them."

The lieutenant is heading in the direction of the university. "I think Tyler would be searching the university some more don't you?' He asks.

"I don't really know, but I guess we can start there." George says.

"There probably won't be many navy blue Mitsubishis around campus this time of year. It should be fairly easy to spot. Would you mind pulling in here so I can grab some breakfast and I'll eat it on the way. Have you eaten yet?" He asks the lieutenant.

"Yes, thanks, I have," the lieutenant says as he's pulling into the drive up.

Lieutenant Sanders orders George's breakfast, picks it up at the next window and returns to the highway and heads to the university.

Chapter Twenty-Two

Samantha's lying naked on the blanket crying, her arms still tied behind her and her clothes are in disarray beside her. She's shaking uncontrollably as Jacob's sitting beside her trying to pull his pants back on as he's staring down at her.

"Samantha, don't cry," he says standing up and turning his shirt right side out. "I was very gentle with you, just like you always liked and I did the things to you, that you would always ask me to do to you before. I didn't want to hurt you, but you wouldn't relax and enjoy it like I was."

"You are a very sick person, Jacob," she cries as she continues to shake. "God will punish you for this."

Jacob kneels down, takes her bra and turns to her. "Sit up and I'll help put your bra back on," he says.

"You've already raped me, Jacob. Can't you at least do the decent thing and untie my hands so I may get dressed on my own?" She asks as she whirls around on her bottom and puts her back to him to expose her tied hands.

"No way, Samantha!" He laughs. "I'm not giving you the slightest chance to come at me again. You are not going to escape. I will help you get dressed," he says as he takes her arm and proceeds to help her stand up. "Bend over, Samantha," he snickers. "So I can fasten this thing for you." He then bends down to pick up her panties while she's struggling to position her bra to fit more comfortably. "Now Samantha, turn around here and we'll put these on." He holds them in front of her about knee high so she may step into them and she does, but not without losing her balance and falls forward into his chest. "Oh Samantha, you liked it so much you want to go another round with me?" He asks.

"Just shut up and get my clothes back on me!" She shouts. "This would be so much simpler if you'd just let me do this myself."

"And then I'd have to untie you," he says. He gets her shorts and top and starts to put them on her, when he hears a vehicle approaching. He runs to the only window in the shed and looks out. He sees that it's a car and he recognizes the make as that of her boyfriend. "Here, Samantha, we have to hurry. It's your boyfriend!" He shouts as he puts her shorts and top back on her in a flash. "Now *you be quiet*," he says as he pulls the knife out and points it at her. *"Or I'll finish you off, too!"*

Chapter Twenty-Three

Tyler locates the shed that the custodian has given him directions to and speeds up. He doesn't immediately see a black SUV. "Please let them be here," he says to himself. He knows that if they are indeed in there, Jacob has already heard him and now has the advantage. He knows Jacob probably has the knife that he killed Amanda with and he wants to make sure Sam doesn't get hurt, that is if she is still alive. Pulling up a little closer to the shed he puts the car in park, but decides not to turn the engine off in case they are in there and he can get away with Samantha and make a break for it. He slouches down around the back of his car in case they are in there and works his way around to the back and there the black SUV is parked. "Yes!" He exclaims to himself.

By now Jacob has Samantha dressed and is standing beside the window, but has pulled the curtain so Tyler can't see him. "I know you are out there, but you'd better not try to get in. I have a knife to Samantha's throat and if you make a move she's dead," he says as he grabs her arm and pulls her over to the window with him. *"Not a word!"* He says putting the knife to her throat.

Her hands are still tied behind her back and she has no other defenses, so she decides to scream anyway. "Tyler, he does have the knife, but I know he won't kill me," she hollers.

"You little slut!" Jacob cries, as he flings her backwards. She catches the heel of her shoe in the blanket and falls hits her head on the concrete floor.

Jacob doesn't try to catch her as she falls and she hits her head on the concrete. She isn't moving, but he couldn't take his eyes off of Tyler, he was coming towards him from outside.

Tyler has to get to Samantha. He didn't care that Jacob had a knife and went for the door full force. He rammed his whole body into it. It stops him cold. *"Damn it!"* He screams. He put both hands on either side of the door, lifts his right leg and kicks the door in, falling into the shed.

Jacob heard the door as Tyler used full force in trying to knock it down.

Jacob hid next to the door so when Tyler bursts through he can attack him from behind.

When Tyler focused, he sees Sam on the floor. He kneels down over her and calls out to her. "Sam, it's Tyler. Can you hear me?"

Before Tyler has time to react, Jacob wraps his arm around him and puts the knife at his throat.

"Don't move, you son of a bitch or I'll kill you!" Jacob screams.

Tyler immediately turns on Jacob and in doing so, Jacob falls back into the pile of helmets, but is able to hang onto the knife.

"I'm going to make you wish you'd never laid eyes on me," Tyler exclaims as he lunges for Jacob who is trying to regain his footing after falling into the helmets. As Tyler grabs him, Jacob's arm goes around Tyler and he plunges the knife into Tyler's back.

"I don't think you're going to hurt anyone," Jacob exclaims as Tyler falls to the floor grabbing Jacob's shirt as he slides down the front of him.

"I will get you!" Tyler says as he loses consciousness, landing on the floor with a heap of blood collecting under him.

Not knowing or caring whether Tyler is dead or alive, Jacob picks Samantha up wanting to get out of there as fast as possible knowing that the police can't be too far behind Tyler. With Samantha over his left shoulder, he looks both ways as he heads towards his SUV. "Yes!" He exclaims out loud. "I may have time to make a run for it and not be seen." Jacob heaves the unconscious Samantha into the passenger's side, sets her upright, closes her door and runs and jumps in and slams his door. "Don't fail me now baby," he says to himself as he reaches in his pocket for the keys, but they aren't there. "Damn it!" He shouts slamming his open hands on the steering wheel. "Where are my freaking keys?" Realizing he had them when he returned with supper, he jumps out of the SUV and returns to the shed. Looking, they aren't lying around anywhere that he can see. "They must have fallen out of my pocket while I was asleep. Samantha, what did you do with my keys?" He asks himself out loud while frantically searching the shed. Kicking Tyler in the side, he starts throwing helmets and the keys come flying out. "Very funny, Samantha!" He says as he retrieves them and runs back out to the SUV.

Slamming the door he manages to pull out from behind the shed and doesn't see a soul in sight. "Well, Tyler where is all your help? Did you indeed think you could snatch Samantha by your own little lonesome? How crazy of you." Jacob's back on the road now and heading for the nearest interstate. Just as he's turning onto the main road of town, Samantha falls towards him and causes him to swerve up over the curb and just misses a light pole. "Damn it, Samantha!" He screams trying to miss the pole, get the SUV back under control and set Samantha back up in the seat.

Chapter Twenty-Four

George is enjoying his breakfast as the two of them slowly canvass the campus for Jacob's SUV, or even better yet Tyler's car.

"George," the lieutenant says. "I use to patrol this area on nights and spent a lot of time talking with the maintenance people. If Jacob worked maintenance while he was here, why don't we go talk to the head maintenance man and see if he can help us."

"Fine," says George as he's wiping grease off of his mouth with the napkin that was in his bag.

George no sooner gets the words out of his mouth and they spot a black SUV driving erratically on the other side of the highway. It jumps the curb and almost hits a light pole before getting back under control and back onto the highway.

"Lieutenant!" George points, throwing his sack on the floor of the squad car. "That's it! That's Jacob's SUV!" He screams pointing in the direction of the SUV. "But if that's Jacob, I don't see Samantha with him."

The lieutenant witnesses the same thing that George does and also notices that the morning traffic on this road is so heavy, that he can't possibly make a turn around and catch him without causing a major accident. He immediately gets on his radio and calls it in.

"Captain, we've located the Black SUV and George suspects it is that of our suspect, but we do not see the girl with him."

He proceeds to give the license number as they watch them in the rearview mirror.

The captain's already sending out an APB on the vehicle to the location. "Lieutenant, we have units on the way, and that license number is a match. Do you know the location of her boyfriend?" He asks.

"That is a negative sir, but I'm sure that he can't be too far behind. From the way he's driving that SUV he thinks that someone is on his tail."

"Proceed with caution Lieutenant," he says. "From your location I'm guessing that they were somewhere on the university grounds overnight. Why don't you canvass that area and see if you spot Tyler and see if he might have the girl with him. He may be in trouble if he's not chasing the SUV.

We'll take care of the SUV, you just see if you can find Tyler. The idiot had no business going after him on his own. I'm getting bad vibes that something may have happened to both of them."

"Yes sir," the lieutenant says. "But please keep us informed on the whereabouts of the SUV."

"Just let us know immediately if they spot the girl in the SUV with the suspect." The lieutenant says.

"Will do," the Captain states. "Over and out."

The lieutenant looks over at George. "Let's go find Tyler."

"I only hope we aren't too late. I can't see Jacob leaving without Samantha can you?"

"No, that was his whole purpose of looking for him. And I'd hate to think that he would kill her too, but you never know. Something isn't right here if Jacob was indeed by himself in the SUV."

Jacob has the SUV under control, glances over to see that Samantha is still out cold when he notices the squad car coming towards him on the other side of the highway. Watching the car, he knows that the officer must have seen him almost hitting the pole and he has his radio mike up to his mouth. "I've got to lose them," he says to himself. No sooner does he say this and he spots the blue interstate sign just up ahead. Stepping on the accelerator he almost rams the car in front of him. "Damn!" He shouts slamming on his brakes. As he approaches the sign he neglects to turn on his right turn signal but waits his turn to make the right hand turn. In making the turn he spots the red lights coming at him with the siren blaring and he accelerates to make a run for it.

"There's the suspect," points the officer as he's talking to his partner.

"I see him too," he says approaching the intersection seeing that he can make the turn and won't have to stop. "Call this in," he says to the officer as he chases the SUV.

"This is car 42 requesting back up," the officer says into the mike.

"Go ahead 42, what is your 10-20?" The voice asks.

"We are heading west at the intersection of Main and First. We've located the suspect and he's making a run for it heading west on the interstate."

"We are sending out units now. Proceed with caution."

The officer puts the mike down and they are in pursuit of the vehicle. "Paul, they said there could be two people in that vehicle, I only see one."

"Yeah, me too, but we must assume that he may have her with him. If she is in there, we don't want her hurt. Steve, he's making a move here. Hang on,

I'm going to try and keep on his tail. If he gets too far ahead we could lose him on an off ramp."

"Car 42, we are in pursuit of the Black SUV and we have him in our sight. What's your 10-20?" The backup officer asks.

"We are right on his tail. I have you in sight. We are going to nail this son of a bitch!" He says.

"Steve, hang on, we are about to make our move!" Paul exclaims as he guns it.

Jacob looks in the rearview mirror to see the squad car getting closer. "Damn it!" He shouts. "What am I going to do now?" He sees the off ramp ahead and makes a break for it. He's in the inside lane, but cuts over without looking back and forces the car in the next lane to hit the guardrail. "Sorry fella," he says to himself as he speeds off the ramp.

"Shit!" Paul says. "He's making it for the off ramp." He checks the rearview mirror to see if he can make his move.

"He made a break for the off ramp." Paul says in the mike to the other squad car.

"We see him. We're getting off the other side and we think we can apprehend him."

Both cars are now on the tail of the SUV and closing in. Jacob doesn't realize that he's about to enter a construction zone on this road.

"Paul, he's just about to the construction zone on this road." Steve says. He gets on the radio to the other car. "Guys. He's just about to hit the construction zone. We can hem him in here. Let's get him."

"Poor sucker!" The officer on the radio answers back. "He's ours now!"

Jacob now sees the construction ahead and realizes that he doesn't have many choices, but he's not about to give up. He sees barricades everywhere, but is determined to make it through. He floors the gas pedal and in doing so doesn't see the dump truck starting to pull in the middle of the road from the left shoulder. He slams on his breaks, but not in time to avoid the truck.

"Look at that son of a bitch! He doesn't see that dump truck pulling back on the road." Paul says just as Jacob hits the right front of the truck and brings him to a dead stop.

Paul gets on the radio and calls for an ambulance knowing full well that there has to be injuries, either to the truck driver or to Jacob.

Chapter Twenty-Five

As the two squad cars are in pursuit of the SUV, the lieutenant and George have located the maintenance supervisor and are on their way to find Tyler, when they hear that Jacob has run into the construction and hit a truck.

"I sure hope that Samantha isn't in that vehicle, Lieutenant," George says as they spot the shed and Tyler's car parked out in front. "There it is!" George shouts.

George is almost out of the squad car before the lieutenant has a chance to put it in park. "Slow down George," the lieutenant says. "Or you're going to get hurt."

"I just have a bad feeling that Tyler is still in there and he's in trouble." George says getting out and slamming the door.

The lieutenant is on the radio calling in that they've spotted Tyler's car.

The door has been left wide open and George tries to run in when the Lieutenant grabs his arm. "George wait. Let me go first," he says as he's taking his gun out of his holster. He also knows that if Tyler and Samantha are in there, it's hard telling what shape they are in and he wants to assess the situation a second before George does. Looking through the doorway, he sees Tyler lying in a pool of blood on the blanket on the floor, but doesn't see Samantha.

"Damn it!" The Lieutenant exclaims as George is peering in behind him.

"Christ!" George says as he pushes past the Lieutenant and kneels down over Tyler. "What has that son of a bitch done to you Tyler? You knew you shouldn't have done this by yourself." George cries, knowing he's really gotten attached to this young man.

The lieutenant reaches over and tries to pull George up. "George, let me see if he's still breathing. George still kneeling moves over and lets the Lieutenant assess Tyler.

"He's still breathing!" The lieutenant exclaims as he is getting up. "I'll call an ambulance. You stay here."

The ambulance arrives in no time, but it seems an eternity to George. The paramedics tell them that it is not good, but if they can get to the hospital soon enough there might be a chance for Tyler. He's lost a lot of blood from the stab wound in the back and his pulse is very shallow. The paramedics quickly start an IV line and oxygen and get him onto the stretcher.

The lieutenant also calls the Captain after calling the ambulance. He tells the Captain that Tyler may not make it and the Captain in turn tells him that Samantha *was* in the SUV with Jacob, that she was tied and was lying down in the seat unconscious from a blow to the head.

The Lieutenant takes George aside while the paramedics continue to work on Tyler and tells him that Samantha was in the SUV and what her status is.

"Will she be alright Lieutenant?" George asks, tears now streaming down his face.

"I think so," the Lieutenant says seeing how upset George is.

"Has anyone contacted Samantha's parents?" George asks. "I completely forgot about them being in town. I've been so wrapped up in finding Samantha and Tyler. I told them I'd get in touch with them this morning before I left the motel."

"The Captain said they called in this morning, when they didn't hear from you. I'm sure they are keeping in touch with them now that they've located Samantha."

They get Tyler in the ambulance as soon as they can and leave for the nearest hospital with their sirens blaring.

There is quite a scene outside when George and the Lieutenant go out. Several of the summer students, maintenance employees and people living close in the neighborhood have gathered.

George thanks the maintenance man and the maintenance man told them that if there was anything they could do to help, just let them know. He reiterated to George what he'd told Tyler, how sorry he was and that this wasn't the Jacob he used to know.

The lieutenant shuts George's door to the squad car, goes around and gets in on the driver's side and they head for the hospital to be with Tyler and Samantha.

"Dear God, I hope the two of them make it Lieutenant," George cries. "I love Samantha like she is my own daughter, and I've become very fond of Tyler too. I could see the connection between the two of them before they even told me."

The lieutenant just shakes his head and concentrates on getting George to the hospital.

Chapter Twenty-Six

The scene at the construction sight is not a pretty one. The officers aren't sure of Samantha's condition. They think maybe she was already unconscious before the accident, since no one had seen her in the SUV. This may or may not have helped her. She has a few cuts on her too and her hands are tied. Unfortunately Jacob hadn't made it. He'd died instantly at the impact of the SUV hitting the dump truck. They aren't surprised, knowing the speed in which he was traveling on impact. The driver of the truck is unconscious and the passenger in the truck with him is in bad shape as well.

It has been quite an eventful day and George is exhausted. The lieutenant stays with him at the hospital as long as he can, but unfortunately has to leave him and file his report before the end of the day. He tells George that he'll come back and check on both Tyler and Samantha later on in the evening. George thanks him for all of his help.

"No need to thank me, George, I was just doing my job," the lieutenant says putting his arm around George and patting him on the back. "Get some rest will you? You look like hell."

"I don't think I will sleep a wink until they tell me how these two are doing. They just have to make it Lieutenant!" George says sounding exhausted.

"Hang in there, I'm sure they'll both be fine" he says and walks out of the emergency waiting area.

Tyler was taken into surgery as soon as he arrived at the hospital and George hasn't heard anything from the doctors yet and it is well into the early evening. It is definitely taking way too long. Samantha is in ICU for observation, but hasn't required any surgery. She has not yet regained consciousness though and the doctors couldn't figure out why. They would only say that she must have had a severe blow to the head. They don't know that the fall on the concrete floor of the shed was the culprit.

George is just about to fall asleep in the chair in the waiting room when he hears someone calling his name. It is Samantha's parents and they are coming towards him.

"George? George?" He hears someone saying and he opens his eyes. It is

Samantha's mother, Marty. "Why do these places always give me the creeps?" George asks himself, as he watches them come towards him from down the long hallway.

"How is she?" George asks. "Is she going to be all right?"

"We just saw her again. She's starting to come around." Marty says. "The doctors are very hopeful that it is just a severe concussion and that she should be fine in a few days. But they say she'll have a whopper of a headache afterwards and that we will have to watch her closely."

"How is Tyler doing?" Asks Curtis, Samantha's father.

"I still haven't heard anything yet. They are still in surgery. It's taking so long and the longer they take the more frightened I become." George says rubbing his hands through his hair and down around his neck. He realizes that all the tension is giving him a headache.

"You look exhausted George." Marty says. "Is there anything I can get you?"

"No, thank you. I couldn't eat anything even if I tried."

"We haven't even had a chance to meet Tyler." Marty remarks. "We were away on holiday when he and Samantha met. She'd called us to see about using the boat over the Fourth and she told me then that she really liked him. She deserves a nice guy. Why did all of this have to happen?" She asks leaning in on her husband's shoulder.

"I only wish that I wouldn't have let the two of them take off on this case," George cries. "It's all my fault."

"George, I know my daughter very well and if I don't miss my guess, I'll bet she begged you to take this case," Curtis says putting his hand on George's shoulder. "Don't do this to yourself. It won't do any of us any good and you couldn't have known all of this was going to happen."

"Yeah, but I could have told her no. Then I had to go and get Tyler into this also. He'd been wanting to come to Palmetto and when Courtney got murdered I saw a great opportunity for him to come and help, knowing that Samantha would be wanting the case and I wouldn't let her do this one alone."

"You couldn't have known it was going to turn out like this George." Curtis says. "You've always taken Samantha's best interests to heart. We don't blame you."

"Honey, we'd better get back to Samantha," Marty says not wanting to stay away from her too long in case she's awake enough to recognize that they are there.

"Will you be alright here by yourself George?" Curtis asks.

"Yes, Yes," George says yawning. "I'll be fine. You two go be with Samantha and if she wakes, up give her my love."

"Please have someone come and tell us as soon as you hear something about Tyler. When Samantha wakes up I'm sure the first thing she will do is ask about him," Curtis says turning away from George and starting back down the hall.

"Thank you, I will," George says as they leave to return to Samantha's room in ICU. "I don't know when I've felt so helpless and alone." He moans to himself. Thinking to himself, he realizes so much has happened that he hasn't reported back to the paper to let them know what has transpired. Getting up was quite a feat considering his exhaustion, but he knows he has to make the phone call. Looking at the big white clock on the wall above the water fountain, he sees that it's too late to contact Lee at the office, so he tries to reach him at home. Lee is very close to Samantha also, almost like a brother to her. The two of them went at it all the time.

Lee answers on the second ring. "Lee, this is George."

"George, we've been anxiously waiting to hear from you. The last time we talked you were going to get some sleep and try to find Samantha this morning. Have you had any luck?" Lee inquires.

"Lee, I'm sorry but we have a bit of bad news," George says running his fingers through his hair. "It's been a really long day and it's about to get longer. Jacob's been caught, however he didn't make it. Samantha and Tyler are both here in the hospital with injuries."

"How bad, George?" Lee asks.

"Tyler's in surgery as we speak and he's been in way too long as far as I'm concerned. He sustained stab wounds in the back. It's going to be touch and go I'm sure. Dear god, I hope he makes it. He just has too," George says with tears welling up in his eyes again.

"I'm so sorry, George, how is Samantha? Is she there with you?" He asks.

"No, Lee, she isn't. She's in ICU for observation. She's still unconscious from a blow to the head. We don't know if the blow to the head occurred when she was held captive, or if it was sustained from the crash."

"Whoa, George!" Lee exclaims making a gesture with his left hand as a stopping motion. "What crash?"

"The police were chasing Jacob on the interstate and as they were about to catch him, he took an off ramp, but didn't know of the construction on the road he was taking and ran into a dump truck. The patrolman said the speed he was going, he hadn't planned on stopping at the construction, but didn't anticipate the dump truck pulling back onto the road and he couldn't miss it.

"Jesus! It's a wonder Samantha made it this far," Lee says. "George are you there alone?"

"Yeah, but I'm okay. But actually, Curtis and Marty are here with Samantha, so I'm not totally alone."

"I can leave right now if you need me."

"No, stay there and take over for me. I need you there now and I can handle this."

"Okay George, but will you call me later and let me know if there have been any changes on those two?" Lee asks and is really concerned about George too. "And don't worry about the time. I want to know if there have been any changes. You know we all think so much of Samantha. She's like a sister/daughter to all of us at the paper. We've seen her grow up from age 16 into a fine, young lady."

"I'll let you know the minute I hear anything," he says and hangs up the phone.

Chapter Twenty-Seven

Dr. Biaca is in with Samantha when her parents return. Hearing the door open, he turns to see Samantha's parents enter. Looking in their eyes he sees very concerned parents and he isn't looking forward to telling them the news he has. "How's Mr. Worth doing? Is he out of surgery?" Doctor Biaca inquires.

"When we left George, Tyler was still in surgery. Just how much longer can it take?" Marty asks.

"It shouldn't be too much longer now, but that depends if they have encountered complications. The location of the stab wounds could be critical to some vital organs in there. But you must hope and pray for the best," he says completing the chart he is writing on. He places the chart on the little desk that is located beside Samantha's bed and turns to Marty & Curtis.

"How's she doing doctor?" Curtis asks concerned. He notices that Samantha isn't making any movement at all like she was earlier. "She looks like she is in a deep sleep."

Sighing Dr. Biaca says. "I'm sorry to have to tell you, but she's just gone deeper into sleep. When you left we thought she was waking up, but obviously she had different ideas. As a matter of fact, the nurse came to get me when she saw that she was not waking and had fallen deeper into sleep. I'm afraid she's gone into a coma."

"A coma!" Marty exclaims wringing her hands. "But we thought she was waking up when we left to check on Tyler! How could this happen?"

"I'm sorry!" The doctor says. "This happens with blows to the head like this and we don't know the extent of the blow. We're getting ready to take her to x-ray now. We're going to do an MRI. Unfortunately Jacob didn't make it or he could be of some help to us. He would know how she sustained the blow. It could have been inflicted by him, a fall or during the accident. The x-rays should tell us more."

Marty is crying now and Curtis is trying to comfort her, but he is just as upset as she is.

"We know you will do what ever to help our daughter, doctor," he says trying to hold his own tears back.

"Why don't you take her home, looking at Curtis, but pointing to Marty. Get some rest and I'll call you with any changes," he states, wishing he could do or say something to ease their pain and worries.

"We live out of town and wish I could take her home, but she won't budge and neither will I. Go ahead and get Samantha to x-ray and we'll wait here. I'll try to get Marty to rest, but I doubt it'll do any good."

"Thank you. I'll let you know as soon as I've had time to read the report," the doctor says, opening the door and motioning for the nurse. "Call and have them come get Miss Summers and take her to x-ray. We need to get some pictures of her head to see what the damage is and maybe that will tell us why she's not coming around."

"Yes, doctor," the nurse says and returns to the front desk on the ICU floor to make the necessary calls.

It's another hour before Tyler's doctor, Dr. Norton, comes to talk to George. George has fallen asleep sitting up, with his head back against the wall. "Sir." Dr. Norton says tapping George on the shoulder.

"Hm?" George asks with a start, opening his eyes. "How's Tyler? Is he okay?

"Whoa, slow down," Dr. Norton says. "I think he's going to be okay. It's going to take some time. He was lucky to have made it at all. He lost a considerable amount of blood and he had a couple serious stab wounds. Fortunately they didn't hit any vital organs, so I think he's going to make it."

"Thank God!" George cries.

"Have you contacted any of Mr. Worth's family? I didn't see a wedding band so I assume that there isn't a wife."

"No, I haven't," George says. "I thought I'd wait to see if he made it."

"You definitely need to do that now," he says. "I'm sure they would be very worried and would want to be here. I will also give them a call to explain his condition. This is going to be a long recuperation and he's going to need a lot of care."

"I'll get in touch with them as soon as possible." George says getting up and extending his arm to shake the doctor's hand. "Thank you so much sir for all you've done."

"You are entirely welcome. Now if you don't mind I want to get back to Mr. Worth," he says. "And by the way, get some rest, you've had quite an ordeal. Are you going to be okay?"

"Yes, I'll be fine when I know Tyler and Samantha will be too. I'll go call Tyler's parents," George says as the doctor turns and heads back to recovery room to be with Tyler. "My instincts tell me this is going to be a long drawn out ordeal." George thinks to himself as he's trying to think of a way to talk to Tyler's parents, once he has the okay to contact them.

Chapter Twenty-Eight

Within the next couple of weeks things had settled down a little, but not like the ones involved had hoped. Bob and Karen had arrived within twenty-four hours of the doctor's phone call and had been there since. They'd spent a lot of time with Tyler and Samantha and were fast becoming good friends of Curtis and Marty Summers. It took Samantha a few more days to come out of her coma and her parents never left the hospital. Their days were spent going from Samantha's room to Tyler's and back. Samantha's doctor was quite sure she would make a full recovery and would be up to her old tricks and back to work in a few more weeks. He'd told her that she'd need plenty of rest. He knew he could probably release her sooner, but with the active life she led, he wanted to make sure he had the controlling thumb. He'd already released her from the hospital after a week.

He'd discussed it with her parents and they agreed. Since she didn't live with them anymore, they wouldn't have near the control and knew she wouldn't do as the doctor ordered. She'd already made too many trips to the hospital to visit Tyler and her parents were afraid of what she might do to her own health. They didn't want to ever again see their daughter lying in a coma.

When Samantha was released from the hospital, Curtis and Marty made the decision to go back to Palmetto. It was hard for them to leave Samantha, but they knew there was nothing else they needed to stay there for. She's a grown woman and Dr. Biaca told them she'd be okay as long as she followed his orders and kept her regular appointments with him. They found her a place to stay so she could be there for Tyler. Not like she was ever going to leave there without him. They could tell that they really loved each other and that's all they could ask for.

Now Tyler was another story. He was going to take a lot of recuperation and therapy. In fact his parents were planning to take him back to Pittsburgh as soon as the doctors say he's able to make the trip. Samantha didn't like the idea, but she knows she has to be realistic about it and that Tyler was going to need a lot of care. She was more than willing to take care of him, but she knew eventually that she would have to go back to work and wouldn't be able to give him the constant care he needed.

It took another week and Tyler's doctor decided there wasn't anything more he could do, that it was time his parents took him back to Pittsburgh. Being in his own surroundings and with his personal physician, whom the doctor had conversed with quite frequently, was what was best for Tyler now.

He'd be leaving on Saturday.

It was Friday night before Tyler left. Samantha had spent her last day with him alone. His parents knew they would be taking him back and he needed to say goodbye to Samantha and her to him. They'd grown fond of her and knew that she would make a great daughter-in-law, but with the circumstances that were with Tyler's present condition of ongoing recuperation and therapy, they didn't know if a young woman like Samantha could withstand the distance that was going to be between them. She has so much life in her they didn't want her to waste it waiting on Tyler to heal. However, if their love now was any indication, nothing was going to keep them apart for long.

"Tyler, I wish I could go with you tomorrow morning," she says, as she's lying next to him in his hospital bed. He's been up several times and even walked up and down the hall corridor, but not without Sam's or the nurse's help.

"I know, Sam." Tyler says tightening his arm around her and planting a soft kiss on her forehead. "Sam, I want you to make me a promise," he says lifting her chin up with his finger so he can look into her eyes. He can see tears welling up and he knows this isn't going to be easy, but he can't live with himself if he doesn't do it for her. "When you return to Palmetto I want you to promise me that you will go on with your life and not wait for me."

"What?" She shouts pushing herself away from him and sitting up. "You can't mean this Tyler."

It is all he can do to retain his composure. "Yes, Sam, I do. You are a young, beautiful and talented woman and I want you to find someone that can make you happy and that you can move on with. It's going to take quite some time for me to be back to normal, if I ever reach that point and I can't do it knowing you are back here waiting and wasting time."

"*No, Tyler*, I will not! *I love you*, and I will be here for you no matter how long it takes for you to get well! We can keep in close contact by phone, e-mail, and I can come to visit you on weekends," she says as the tears are streaming down her face. " I can't let you push me away like this! I won't Tyler!"

"There will be no more discussion on it, Sam." Tyler says, trying to put up a good front but getting a big lump in his throat knowing what he is about to say next is going to take it's toll on him. "We've had some really great times, but now that the case has been solved and Jacob can't be a threat to anyone anymore, my job is done and I must get back to Pittsburgh, get myself healed and return to my job there, if I indeed will still have one when the time comes."

Samantha is crying uncontrollably now and Tyler isn't sure he can hold together much longer looking into her sad eyes and knowing how much he really loves her. "Please go now, Sam, and don't come back in the morning. I don't think it would be a good idea. It will only be that much harder on you," he says wiping the tears that are starting to run down his cheeks.

"Tyler, please!" Sam begs. "You don't mean this," she says falling on his chest forgetting momentarily about his wounds.

"Ow!" Tyler screams.

"I'm so sorry, Tyler," Sam cries, moving off his chest trying not to hurt him further. "Please don't make me go."

"Samantha, I've made up my mind and I think it's time for you to go. And I'd really appreciate it if you wouldn't try to contact me either."

Samantha was almost in shock as she starts to move off of Tyler's bed. He could see it and he wishes like hell that he didn't have to do this and wonders if he can live with him- self for doing it, but he had to, for her sake.

"I will always love you Tyler Worth! And I will never understand why you are doing this to me! *Damn you!*" She screams, grabs her purse from the chair and opens the door. Before leaving she turns once more and Tyler has turned his back to the window so he can't see her walk out the door. That would have been too much for him to bear.

Once out the door, Samantha doesn't know which way to turn. She feels like her life has just ended right before her eyes and that someone has just punched her in the stomach. She feels so empty. She'd rented a car once she was back on her feet, since hers was back in Palmetto. She walks to it now, unlocks the door and slides in. Staring out the windshield she breaks down and puts her head on the steering wheel saying out loud. "Tyler, I love you, but I won't let this keep me down. If this is what you want, this is what you will get!"

She cries uncontrollably until no more tears will fall and then forces herself to start the car.

Once Tyler is sure she's gone, he turns over in his hospital bed and stares at the ceiling with tears still streaming down his face. "What the hell did I just do? I will never love anyone like I love her, but yet I just let her walk out that door. I hope to God that one day she will understand why I did what I had to do." He knew he would definitely miss her and it would be a hell of a long time before he would get over her, if ever.

His parents come to get him the next morning. He'd previously spoken with them and told them what he was going to tell Sam. They knew it was going to be the hardest thing he'd had to do in his life and they were supporting him even though they know he loves her. They didn't know till they walked into his room whether he'd be able to follow through with it. But they knew immediately. He looks like death warmed over.

"Tyler," his mother says while walking over beside him. "Are you sure you did the right thing? You look like you just lost your best friend."

"I did, Mom," Tyler says with the tears welling up in his eyes again. He hadn't slept at all and he is feeling really lousy about what he's done. "Can we just get out of this place and go home?"

"Sure son," his father says as he grabs Tyler's bag. "Time will heal a lot of things. You've been through enough. Let's get going," he says as he puts his hand under Tyler's elbow to help him to the door.

Doctor Norton opens the door just as they start to open it and see that he's pushing the wheelchair that is to take Tyler down to the front entrance.

"Aren't there volunteers to do this?" Curtis asks.

"Yes, but this time I want to do it myself," he says as he motions for Tyler to climb on. "Tyler are you sure you are up to this?" And he notices the tears in Tyler's eyes.

"Yeah, I guess so. I had a rough night saying goodbye to Samantha and I didn't sleep last night, but I'll be okay."

"She's one hell of a lady!" Doctor Norton says, starting to push Tyler out into the hall and not knowing what has happened between the two of them. "I'm sure you are going to miss her."

He can't see Tyler crying as he pushes him to the elevator.

Chapter Twenty-Nine

It's been almost two months. Samantha's been back to work for most of it and George is really concerned about her. She hasn't gotten back to her old self and he's noticed that she's lost some more weight. She'd lost some during her ordeal but he could see she was getting thinner. She's buried herself in her work, but it isn't helping. He knows she's thinking of Tyler all the time. There are many times when he goes by her office and sees her staring out the window. When she'd turn around he would see the tears in her eyes.

Today is no exception. "Samantha, you just can't stop thinking about Tyler, can you?"

Turning away from the window, she looks at George with those sad eyes. "I just called again to see if he'd talk to me. It's been almost two months and he still refuses to even speak with me on the phone. His mother's run out of excuses for him not coming to the phone, and sometimes she just tells me the truth and says he doesn't want to speak to me. I know this is hard on her having to do this to me, but she is only following his wishes. Today was exceptionally bad though. Tyler is moving back into his place this weekend. Karen just told me that he's doing much better and it's time he moved back. He's well enough now that it's getting to be too close quarters for the three of them."

"That's great news, Sam," George says walking over by the window closer to her.

"I'm sorry George, of course it's good news. It's just that if he's doing so well why hasn't he contacted me?"

What George isn't telling her and can't, is that he's been keeping in close contact with Tyler ever since they released him from the hospital and took him home. She doesn't know that Tyler is blaming himself for what happened. He believes very strongly that if he hadn't suggested that they go to the university, things would have been different and none of this would have happened.

"Samantha, sometimes things happen for a reason. You are going to have to try to get over him and move on. Now I know you've had a few dates with

Todd. How are they going?" By mentioning Todd, he thinks maybe it will get her mind off Tyler.

Todd Blair is another aspiring journalist that hired in about the same time Samantha did at the *Tribune*. George knows that he to has a crush on Samantha but never said anything to pursue getting them together because he tries to stay out of peoples personal lives. He has enough to handle with just the paper, let alone playing cupid. Besides Samantha was going with Jacob at the time and Todd was totally into his work there. However, now was a different story. He hadn't approached Todd at first regarding Samantha after she returned, but water cooler talk always gets started and spreads like wildfire. Besides Lee kept everyone informed while he was away and he's sure Lee told them more about what was going on than just the accident. Of course you didn't have to be a rocket scientist to see that Tyler and Samantha had a thing going.

Walking away from the window Samantha turns her leather chair around and sits back down. Leaning back she rolls her head over in George's direction. He's sitting down in an arm chair on the front side of her desk and is waiting to hear about her date.

"George, I know you have done your very best to help me, I'm not blind nor stupid. I'm well aware that you are the one that set me up with Todd. He's a very nice man and I think a lot of him. In fact we've become pretty good friends. He's been very understanding."

"That's great, Sam," he says putting his elbows on the chair arms, interlocking his fingers and crossing his legs. "Is there a chance you could become more than just friends?" George asks knowing full well he's probably treading on thin ice in asking too many questions and this is territory unbecoming of a boss, but he and Samantha are so close he thinks of her as the daughter he doesn't have. He also knows full well that Sam will tell him immediately when he's overstepping his bounds.

"George, sometimes you know me better than my own parents. Of course you see more than they do, because we're here all day every day together."

"So are you telling me things are going pretty good with you two?"

Glancing at her watch Samantha then looks back at George. "If you have a few more minutes George, I need to talk to someone about this."

"I'll make time," he says and at the same time gets up to go close the door to her office. It's late Friday and he just has a couple things left to wrap up before the weekend. "What's going on, Sam?" He asks returning to sit back down.

"George, It's obvious that Tyler doesn't want to have anything to do with me anymore, but I also know he still loves me. And that's the hardest part. How can I move on with another relationship, when I know in my heart how we care for each other? It's not fair to either of us, and it's certainly not fair to Todd."

None of this makes any sense. If he's moving back into his place he must be doing okay. It's not that his health is keeping him away from me anymore."

"Sam, I don't have any answers. But it seems to me that if this is what Tyler wants, then you will just have to live with it and move on." George says sounding like a typical male and obviously not letting on to her that he already knows the reason. "Does this mean that there may be a connection between you and Todd?"

"Maybe," she says bowing her head looking down at her hands feeling a little guilty. "We've had some really good times on the few dates we've had. But I can honestly say I haven't given Todd a fair chance. I really thought I loved Jacob. Then falling in love with Tyler was something really special. I realized then that I wasn't really in love with Jacob. Do you think that I could fall in love again, knowing how I feel about Tyler and not getting the chance to, play it out, as they say?"

"Samantha, you are asking the wrong guy that question." George says, his face turning a little red. "I'm no Ann Landers."

Samantha laughs at George's remark and that's the first time he's heard that out of her in quite a while. Maybe there is hope for her after all. She deserves so much, it is killing him to see her go through this. He knows he will be talking to Tyler again, soon, and Tyler will be fishing for more information on her.

But will he really be ready for the answers?

"There is nothing else I would like more, than to get my life back in order, George. But it still hurts so much whenever I think of Tyler, which is most of my waking hours."

"Rome wasn't built in a day Samantha. Why don't you give it a little more time? Maybe something just as special will develop between you and Todd. But if not, it's a beginning and you will find someone again, that I'm sure of. Any guy would be lucky to get you. You are an intelligent, fun loving, easy going young lady and given the right time, place and person, you will move on."

"Thank you for the encouragement George," Samantha says as she walks around her desk to give George a hug. "However, I don't know if I'll ever be over Tyler. There is just something down deep that tells me we are meant to be together."

Rising from his chair George takes Samantha in his arms and gives her a big bear hug.

"Give it time girl, give it time. I need to get back to my office Samantha. If you need to talk again please just holler."

"Thank you, you know I will," she says and backs away so he can go back to work and knows she must do the same.

Just as George is leaving Samantha's office, Todd is coming down the hall.

"Hello, Todd. Are you needing to see me?" George asks knowing that Todd isn't usually in this area unless he's coming to see him.

"No, I'm not George, I came down to see Samantha," Todd says as he points in the direction of her office.

George looks and sees that Samantha is settling back to work at her desk. "Todd, if you have a few minutes I'd like to speak with you." Knowing full well that he should be minding his own business, he asks him anyway.

"Yes, I have. Just give me a minute to say something to Samantha and I'll be right in."

Entering Samantha's office Todd can see that she's been crying again. It hasn't been easy for him, but it wasn't for the lack of trying. He, like everyone else at the paper, knows what she's been going through and at first he'd just been trying to be a good friend but it was fast becoming more than that for him. But he also knows that if Tyler should show up on her doorstep, he would have no chance in hell with her, nor would anyone else.

"Samantha, are we still on for tonight?" Todd asks hanging onto the doorknob leaning into her office.

"Oh, hi, Todd. I didn't see you there," she says wiping a tear off her cheek. It's Friday night and she's about to close up for the weekend. "Sure, I'm game if you are," she says trying to get herself back together. She really likes Todd and giving him half a chance, she knows she could grow even more fond of him. But could she be fair to him? She doesn't want to hurt anyone the way she is hurting and if there is ever a chance for her and Tyler, Todd would no longer be in the picture.

"Good. I'll be at your place at seven, is that okay with you?"

"Fine, I'll be ready," she smiles.

"See you then, Samantha. George needs to see me, so I'll be there at seven," he smiles back, closes her door and walks over to George's office.

Knocking on George's door, he motions for Todd to come on in as he's looking for the paperwork that he wants to go over one more time before the weekend. George doesn't like loose ends and then having to come in to them on Monday morning. In this business Monday morning may not be what you'd expect, depending on what transpires over the weekend. A news-breaking story may take precedence over what you were working on Friday.

"Have a seat Todd, this will only take a minute. I know it's Friday and you, like everybody else, want to get out of here on time."

"Thanks for the consideration, George. I do have a date with Samantha at seven," he says sitting down in one of the cushy chairs in George's office, wishing he had just one of these in his office.

"That's what I'd like to talk to you about Todd, if you don't mind me not minding my own business. In fact I was just talking to Samantha about you. She's still hurting very much, as I'm sure you know. I wish there was something I could do for her, but I nor anyone else can at this point. Only be there for her. But my concern right now is you, Todd. She told me that the two of you have been together a few times. Do you mind me asking how you feel about her?" He asks knowing full well this is none of his business and he is now stepping over the line. "You can tell me to mind my own damn business if you want and I'll understand."

"No, it's okay. At first I was only trying to be a friend, but with Samantha it's too easy for it to be more. She is the type of girl that doesn't just go out with guys for the sake of having a good time. She has a heart and she realizes that other people have feelings too. I keep telling myself that I'm only feeling sorry for her, but I know that isn't true. With me it's quickly becoming more than that."

"That's just what I was afraid of Todd. And it's my fault for getting you involved in this. You'd think after all that's happened I'd keep my nose out of things, but she's like a daughter to me and I can't stand to see her hurting. If I'd left Tyler in Pittsburgh in the first place none of this would have happened," he says feeling guilty again.

"Oh George. You can't be blaming yourself for what happened to them. It wasn't your fault. They were all just doing their jobs, and if you'd known anything like this was going to happen, you never would have put them on the case."

"But I do, and that's the point. Now I am being so protective of her I think I am trying to help too much and someone else may get hurt in the process. I don't want it to be you."

"I'm a big boy George, I can take care of myself," Todd says smiling. "I know what you are thinking and believe me I've gone over it a thousand times in my mind too. Now why don't you quit worrying about her and let things take their course? She's a strong woman and she'll work her way through this. It isn't going to be easy, but I plan on helping the process, if you know what I mean."

"Okay. But please watch your step. She's still very vulnerable Todd," George says cautioning him.

"Thanks for the warning. Now have a nice weekend and I'll try to do the same. I'm going to spend as much time with her as she will allow me. Do you blame me?"

"No, I can't blame you a bit. Have a good weekend and I'll see you next week," he says standing to shake Todd's hand and shooing him out of his office so he can go back to looking for the file he was looking for before Todd came in.

Chapter Thirty

It was going to be a great weekend. He'd proven all of the doctors wrong, in how long the recovery process would be. They couldn't believe he did it so quickly. And now he has to prove to his parents he is ready to be on his own once again. Tyler's moving back to his place and not soon enough to please him. If he'd had his way about it he'd have been back home sooner. He is tired of being waited on hand and foot. He needs some space. Not that he doesn't appreciate his parents taking care of him, he does. It is just that he needs time alone to think and reflect back on all that has happened. He knows his parents aren't exactly pleased with how he ended it with Sam, but he felt at the time he was doing what was best for her. But what was best for her was not necessarily best for him. It has been a horrific couple months and he feels like shit. He isn't proud of what he's done at all. But he didn't do it because he wanted to.

"Tyler, George is on the phone for you," Karen calls from the kitchen. Tyler heard the phone ring, but knew his mother would get it. She's been in the kitchen baking cookies for him to take home Saturday, when he moves back. He told her she didn't need to do this, but he knows how moms are. They can't seem to spoil you enough. So he usually just lets her do her thing.

"Thanks, Mom, I'll get it in here," he says picking up the receiver. "Hi, George what's up?"

"How ya doing, Tyler? He asks. "I hear you're moving back to your place tomorrow. That's great, but are you sure you are up to it?"

"George, you don't know how I'm looking forward to this. It's time I am on my own again." he says sitting down in the plaid lounge chair that is next to the table the phone is on. He still can't stand too long without his back hurting. The stab wounds are still very adamant in letting him know they are still there, doing even the simplest tasks. They let him know immediately that some of the pain is still there and he needs to sit down. Looking at his watch he notices the time. "George it's Friday night. Are you calling from the office?"

"I'm finishing up some loose ends. I don't like to have unfinished business staring me in the face come Monday morning."

"Sounds good. How's Sam, George?" Tyler questions. Just mentioning her name gives him an empty feeling in his gut. To this day he still sees the look on her face when she walked out of his hospital room. It was the worst day of his life. "I've really been concerned about her since our last conversation. Have you had a chance to talk with her?"

"Yes, Tyler, as a matter of fact I have. I was just in and had a talk with her this afternoon before I called you. Seeing that pretty young lady as devastated as she is, is heartbreaking. But Tyler, I have to tell you she isn't going to wait around for you forever. You do understand that don't you?"

"That's exactly why I said to her what I did George. I didn't want her waiting around for me. Seeing her and knowing she could have been killed because we went off half cocked to do this story, is something I will never be able to live with. She deserves someone better than me. No matter how much I still love her, I can't put her through anything like that ever again. I didn't want her to think she had to take care of me the rest of her life. I didn't realize at the time that my recovery would be so fast and I'd be back on my feet. I just wanted her to go back to Palmetto and resume her life. She has a great future ahead of her."

"I understand where you are coming from Tyler, but are you sure you are ready for her to go on with her life?" George asks knowing he isn't going to be ready for what he is going to say next.

"What are you getting at George?" Tyler asks.

"Tyler, Sam's started seeing someone else," he says knowing that if he doesn't miss his guess, this is going to hit Tyler right where it hurts the most, in the heart.

There is complete silence on the other end of the line. "Tyler are you still there?"

"Yes, I'm still here. I knew you were going to tell me something like this sooner or later, but I'd just assumed it would be much later," he says feeling the sick feeling in his stomach and it isn't from the wounds this time. "You know how much I love her and this really hurts. Who is the lucky guy and is there any chance that it's serious?"

"I won't tell you the guy's name. If you are that interested and want to know, you'll have to get that information from Samantha. But I suggest that if you still love her, you'd better do something about it and soon. Like I said, she isn't going to wait around for you forever. And even though I know she loves you too, I don't know that she would even consider having you back."

"She's better off George," he says staring out the window across the room. Of course this isn't what is going through his mind, but he is going to have to live with his decision if it kills him–and it just might. "Thanks for calling me George. I really appreciate all of your concerns where Sam and I are concerned. You are the one that put us together. Do you realize it's only been a few short months ago? So much has happened, that it seems like a lifetime."

"Don't remind me. I think about it every time I see that pretty face of hers. If it hadn't been for me, none of this would have happened. But I'm the one that didn't think she could handle this one on her own. I had to send for you to come down here and then look what happened."

"George it's not your fault, I fell in love with her."

"I know, but it doesn't make me feel any better. Well I need to go. I just wanted to bring you up to date and then let you decide on your own, what to do with the information. But don't wait too long, if you decide you want her back. Take care and keep me posted on how you are doing."

"Thanks George, I will. You did what you thought was best in calling me. Now I just have to live with it," he says resting his head in his left hand, suddenly feeling very tired, he hangs up the receiver.

It's quite a while before Tyler realizes how long he's been sitting there staring out the window. Looking at his watch it's almost six thirty. But time doesn't matter anymore. He's just about to lose the woman he truly loves, for good. But he's made his decision and even the phone call from George doesn't change anything. He can't go back and interrupt Sam's life again. She would find happiness, he was sure of that.

Tyler knows he will have to go on with his life also and being the sort of gentleman he is, he'd rather be dying on the inside than to go back on his word now. He will live with what he's done. It might take a while but things will get better.

Chapter Thirty-One

Samantha's mulling over her talk with George while she's getting ready for her date with Todd. She really does care for him. He's very kind, good looking and compassionate. Todd's about six foot one, with light brown hair and beautiful dark blue eyes.

And she must say that he has a great body that isn't hard to look at either. But the one thing that impresses Samantha the most is how he handles the situation with Tyler. He knew before he'd ever asked her out what he would be up against. At first he became a good friend. He told her he just wanted to be there for her, if she wanted to talk. He told her George had explained the situation in detail when he approached him about her. He'd admired her work and wanted to get to know her other than on the professional level and when she returned to work he thought maybe it would be a good time. It wasn't easy for either of them the first few times they talked. At first Samantha thought Todd was there for the rebound, but she quickly found out that was not who he was. In the last few weeks even though they hadn't dated but a few times, he has stopped by her place several times after work just to talk and be her shoulder to cry on.

Looking at her watch she realizes she only has about an hour left before he arrives. She is fixing a nice dinner at home this evening. They are having steak and shrimp on the grill, a nice salad and the night before she'd made a cheesecake. She figures he can help cook on the grill and they can eat whenever they wish. Everything is ready, except for grilling the meat and shrimp. It's a beautiful evening and she hopes he'll take her for a walk on the beach. She'd been down to her favorite spot on the beach after work like she's accustomed to and had done a lot of soul searching. After her talk with George this afternoon, she'd made a decision.

Looking in the mirror one last time, Samantha wants to make sure she looks just right. She'd told Todd to dress casually so she doesn't want to be over dressed herself. Being dressed up five days a week was enough, so when it comes to weekends, it's casual dress for her. She doesn't mind dressing up, but that just isn't her. She prefers dressing grungy. A pair of shorts and a t-shirt is almost always her weekend wear. But for tonight she put on her yellow denim Capri's and a short-sleeved navy top with three quarter length sleeves.

As she's stepping into her navy flats, the doorbell rings. Glancing at her watch it is seven on the dot when she opens the door. Todd's standing there looking handsome as usual. It is hard to focus anywhere but on his eyes, but she does manage to notice he has dressed casually and he looks very smart in his khaki slacks and cream polo style shirt. Like everyone else in Palmetto, he's acquired a great tan from the summer. She also mentally notes that it would be a shame for him to lose that tan when it fades this fall.

"Hello, Samantha," he says as he smiles.

"Hi. Come on in. Did you have a nice drive out here?" She asks knowing how he likes taking drives by the ocean.

"Yes, I did." But right now he isn't thinking much about his drive down, but how she looks in those Capri's.

"And I must say you look fantastic this evening. Those yellow Capri's look great on you." Most men wouldn't know what Capri's are, but he's very fashion conscious and you can tell by the way he dresses. He's always in fashion.

"Thank you," she says blushing, as she heads for the kitchen to get the bottle of wine. "Would you like to pop the wine?"

"Sure, just give me the corkscrew?"

Opening the drawer and getting the corkscrew for him she asks. "Would you like to take a walk on the beach before dinner or are you starved? Everything is ready except for grilling the steak and shrimp, so we can eat anytime."

"No, I can wait. I had a late lunch today because of the story I was working on, so let's take a walk first. There aren't going to be too many evenings left that are this warm. Before long with fall coming, we'll be wearing our jackets," he said noticing that she is a lot more relaxed than when he saw her in her office this afternoon. Driving down here this evening he wondered what kind of mood she'd be in when he arrived.

"Good let's go then."

It is a great evening to take a walk. The beach is mostly deserted except for a few late vacationers and locals. They walk side by side down the beach close enough to the water to get their feet wet, but not deep enough to get his slacks. Of course he'd already rolled his pant legs up and they'd left their shoes on the back porch.

PALMETTO SUMMER

They drink their wine and make small talk at first, about how their week went. Then Samantha decides it's time she speaks what's been on her mind the entire day. "Todd, may I be frank with you?"

A little shocked Todd looks over at her. "Sure, what's on your mind?" As he takes her hand in his and continues to walk the beach.

"I've been doing quite a lot of thinking lately. I know you've been very patient with me and I really do appreciate it. You've been a great friend and you've helped me through some really rough times where Tyler is concerned."

"Yeah, so what's your point?" He asks being a typical male.

"Hear me out here okay? This isn't an easy decision for me." she says looking up into those eyes.

"I'm sorry, continue. I won't say another word," he says becoming a little worried about what she is about to say. He doesn't know that maybe she's been in contact with Tyler and she's going to give him his walking papers.

"I'm sure you saw that I'd been crying again when you stuck your head in my office today. I'd just had a talk with George. He's not only my boss, he's also a very good friend," she feels her hand getting sweaty in his, because she's suddenly getting very nervous. "Sometimes parents can't be objective when it comes to their own, so I use George. I make it hard on him sometimes, but he can handle it. I actually think he enjoys it sometimes, but don't tell him I said that. He's been a life saver for me since our ordeal."

"He's a great guy." Was all Todd would say.

"He told me today that maybe it is time for me to move on. I will always love Tyler, Todd. I don't have any answers because he won't talk to me and that is what is hardest. But after this long and if he's well enough to move back home and be on his own, if he really wanted me he'd made an effort before now. So I guess what I'm saying is, that it's time for me to let him go."

Todd can see that this isn't an easy decision for her. Tears welling up in her eyes.

"I've grown fond of you Todd, but I haven't been fair. I haven't let you really into my life. I've kept you at arms length, hoping that Tyler would come to his senses. I know this sounds like I'm rebounding but actually I'm not." She stops him by putting her hand on his stomach. "Todd, I'd like to pursue this relationship further, if you'll have me. I know it may not be easy for you, because you'll be thinking Tyler will always be there in the way. Can you help me to do this? I need to get on with my life."

A little stunned at first, he doesn't quite know what to say. He takes her in his arms and holds her planting a kiss on her forehead. "Samantha, I never thought in a million years this was what you were going to say. I knew there was a possibility that you were going to stop seeing me, because of your feelings for Tyler, but not this. You have just thrown me a curve. Samantha, I do care for you a great deal, but—" And he stops what he is about to say.

Looking up at him Samantha knows she's said the wrong things. "Todd I'm sorry, but I had to say how I feel. Are you upset with me?"

"No, Samantha, I'm not upset with you. But you have to realize if I further this relationship with you, I'm going into it knowing Tyler will always be there. Do you think that is a good basis for a relationship?"

He asks moving her away from him so he can look her in the eyes. He wants to see if he can read them and if she really means what she is saying.

"Probably not. But how else am I going to know if I can get over him unless I move on?"

"I don't have all the answers either Samantha, but I do know this," he says, knowing that he is going to have to be very careful how and what he is going to say next. Extending his arms out and placing his hands on her upper arms, he continues taking a deep breathe. "Samantha, I may be a fool for doing this, but I strongly believe that in time I will help you forget him. I want you to know though, that I won't be a crutch or a stand in. If this is really what you want, I'll try. God knows I want to be a lot more in your life than just a good friend," he says and pulls her towards him, puts his arms around her and kisses the top of her head. "God help me, Samantha, if I'm doing the wrong thing for both of us. I couldn't stand to see you hurting again."

Samantha looks up into his eyes as he lowers his lips to hers and they stand there, for what seems like an eternity kissing. She ignites fire into Todd like he's never felt before. Samantha feels a little of it too, however, it's not as strong as Todd's. Would it ever be she didn't know, but she now feels that she is sure going to try as he starts to move his hands under her top and caress her back, sending a tingling sensation up her back. She moves closer into his chest and tightens her arms around his neck in response. And right then neither one of them cares who is on the beach. As far as they are concerned it is just the two of them.

Coming to his senses and forcing his lips from hers he says to her regretfully after what seems an eternity, "Don't you think we should be heading back up to your place?

There are more people on this beach than just us and they are starting to point and stare." Seeing the fire in her eyes at that moment, he knows there is no way he is going to douse that flame. Knowing the area as well as she does, because he's lived here all his life also, he grabs her hand. "Come on I know a place."

"Oh you do, do you?" She says smiling and they head up the beach towards the cove a little less than a quarter mile more. On the way she wonders if this isn't moving too fast, but she isn't about to throw this moment away. She's had two heartbreaks and she isn't about to have another one. If this is moving too fast, so be it. She deserves some happiness and if Todd is willing to give her the chance, she isn't about to pass it up.

The cove is a very secluded place. It isn't a spot tourists visit. The locals are very careful to save this spot for themselves. But couples have been coming here for many years to be alone. It is their very own piece of paradise and rightfully so. Sand dunes have formed their own wall with palm trees, hibiscus and crepe myrtle, to form the seclusion creating the perfect romantic location. Even in the summer it is cool here because the trees and foliage shelter it from the sun, and it receives the continuous breeze off the ocean. But this evening is perfect. The hot summer evenings are gone.

Luckily when they arrive it is unoccupied. It's the most beautiful place on the beach, and as far as Samantha's concerned, is the most beautiful place in all of Palmetto.

Not having brought a blanket, Todd takes off his shirt and puts it down on the sand for Samantha. "How sweet, but you don't have to do that for me. I'm use to sitting in the sand," she says nervously.

Noticing the nervousness in her voice he puts his fingers over her lips to hush her, sets down on the sand and pulls her down with him, making sure she lands on his shirt. "I won't do anything you don't want me too." He says as he lays her down and gently places one of his arms over the top of her, so he's looking into her eyes. Not wanting to move too fast he kisses her lightly, then keeps his face close to hers to see if it relaxes her any.

She smiles, pulls him down to kiss him and wraps her arms around his neck.

Todd takes his cue from there and slowly starts removing her t-shirt from inside her pants while gently kissing her. He feels her take a sharp breath as he works his hand up to her breast. The kiss becomes harder as he rolls her towards him to undo the back of her bra. She's not stopping him as he lets her lie back down as he softly begins cupping her breast with his hand. She begins arching her back a little towards him in rhythm with his hand. The t-shirt's a little binding, so he pulls it up over her breasts to remove it. She sits up to make the removal easier.

It isn't completely dark yet and he gets a good look. "God you're beautiful," he says looking at her and at the same time lies her back down. She smiles again, blushing a little and he kisses her.

"Samantha, I won't do anything you don't want me to," he says again, hoping she doesn't stop him now.

At this moment, there is no one on this earth, but the two of them. Looking into his eyes she says, moving yet closer to him. "Will you make love to me?"

"Yes," he says seeing that fire in her eyes again and feeling it in him. They can't possibly be pried apart. While kissing her, he takes the hand that is caressing her breast and slowly descends down her stomach, undoes her belt and zipper and slowly cups the soft mound below.

Before realizing it, her pants are removed and he's taking off his owns slacks nervously. Straddling on top of her, he gently uses his right knee to part her legs. Lying down on top of her and kissing her, his manhood can no longer resist and he enters her. He keeps telling himself he wants this to go slow, as not to hurry it, but human nature takes over. The feel inside of her heightens all of his senses. There is no more waiting, as their rhythm is in sync and they climax together. Their bodies spent, Todd rolls over to lie down beside her and the ocean breeze feels so cooling on their damp bodies.

"Samantha," he says nuzzling her neck.

"Shsh," she says hushing him. He can't see her smiling because it's now gone completely dark.

"Thank you." She says not wanting to spoil the moment for either of them and doesn't want him apologizing for anything. As far as she's concerned it couldn't have been more perfect. Just maybe, she's going to be able to forget Tyler after all.

The walk back to her place is very quiet. Neither of them feels they need to say anything. But as they approach her house, Todd's feeling very hungry. "Samantha, are you going to feed me or let me starve?" He asks feeling his stomach rumble. So much is going through his mind right now he knows if he dwells on it too long it will spoil it. He's going to enjoy what they have right now. It's already more than he could have asked for.

Todd takes over grill duties while Samantha finishes getting things ready in the kitchen. Their dinner is great and they both eat like they haven't eaten in days, even though Todd had already eaten a sizeable late lunch. But he's rather shocked at how much she eats, because he knows she's been eating next to nothing and it was taking its toll on her.

He'd help her clear the table but she tells him they'll just leave everything and she'll take care of it later. There's no hurry with tomorrow being Saturday.

"Want to have our coffee out on the porch?" She asks walking from the kitchen back into the dining room.

"Sure, sounds good to me," he says taking a cup from her, getting up from the table and heading towards the door that goes out to the porch.

"I love the end of summer." She says taking a sip of her coffee trying not to spill any, while she's trying to maneuver the swing. "It's like a breath of fresh air after the summers have been so hot."

Todd knows she's making small talk, so he'll go along with it, but at some point he's going to bring up what took place earlier. "I think you have to live here to appreciate the summers. Most vacationers are here for a short while to soak up all of the ocean and rays they can, and then go home to what they call 'reality'. This is reality for us and I can't imagine leaving it. Those winters up north must really be awful."

"I don't ever plan on finding out," she says looking out over the black ocean that the moon and stars have illuminated.

"Samantha, we need to talk." Was all he would say taking another sip of his coffee.

"Do we really have to?" She asks knowing full well what about.

"No, we don't, but we are going to," he says, not wanting to spoil the evening, but he needs to know what's going on in that pretty little head of hers. "Now that you've had a chance to think about it, are you sorry?"

Setting her empty cup down on the porch railing, she leans back against the swing turning towards him bringing her left leg up into the swing and sitting on it. Taking a hold of his hand she says. "Todd, I can only imagine what is going through your mind right now. You are probably wondering, one if I think you took advantage of me, two if I regret it and three will I ever want to see you again. I'm sure you know by now that if I thought you'd taken advantage of me, I would have gotten furious during or afterwards and sent you on your way. After all, I don't think I used any resistance myself. And if you think for one moment, that I thought of Tyler during that time you are sadly mistaken. I'd already told you I wanted to move on and I meant it. That time with you was absolutely phenomenal," she says smiling at him and squeezing his hand. "Was it a little to soon, maybe, but it happened. I think you have just given me what I needed and shown me that I can go on. I know it won't be easy, especially for you. But please believe me when I say,

I want to further this relationship with you and see where it leads." Not saying a word at first, he pulls her closer, wraps his arms around her and kisses her, exploring every inch of her mouth. He can't seem to get enough of her and at that thought she nuzzles against him and he's ready for more. "Samantha, I couldn't be happier," he says finally breaking for air and decides not to say anything more. Actions speak louder than words, and for now that is enough for him.

Chapter Thirty-Two

Tyler's move back into his place went without a hitch and he's been back for a few months now and is almost completely recovered. A few twinges now and then but otherwise he's doing better than expected. He was allowed to return to work in his Pittsburgh office the first of December. They were glad to have him back and he was particularly glad to be there. Upon his return he'd dove head first into his work. He felt that it was the best medicine to help him get over Sam. The work helped during the day while he was at the office, but when it was time to go home, that was another story. It was the emptiest place on earth for him. After spending as much time with her as he did while he was in Palmetto, then coming back to Pittsburgh and living with his parents, he thought solitude was what he wanted. Well he was wrong. The more he was alone the more he missed Sam. He'd gone out on a few dates, but most of them never seemed to work out. He knew it wasn't their fault. He did see one of them a few times and her name was Jill. She was the only one that remotely made him forget Sam, but he couldn't see any sexual attraction. He was always comparing her to Sam and he finally broke it off with her also. She was heartbroken because she had really fallen for him, but she also knew that his head was messed up with Samantha. He'd explained everything to her up-front, but she thought she was the one to make him forget. Obviously she was wrong. It wasn't a nasty breakup, but Tyler regretted ever getting in the relationship in the first place.

In November George had called him to check in and asked him if he'd like to come to Palmetto and help do another major investigative story. He'd politely said no to George not wanting to be near Sam. He knew at the first sight of her he would crumble and he wasn't about to put her through it. Besides, George was keeping him up to date on her and she seemed to be getting along just fine with her new boyfriend. In fact he'd said things were getting pretty serious. She'd done just what he thought he wanted her to do and that was to move on with her life. He couldn't just come waltzing back in and expect her to come running back. However, that was exactly what he wanted. He'd had plenty of time to think and now he knows he's made the biggest mistake of his life. Looking back, he let his emotions of everything that happened and his injuries override his heart.

It's Monday night and he's watching "Monday Night Football" from his favorite lounge chair. He'd just put up his Christmas tree over the weekend and the light from it and the TV are all that is illuminating the room. The snow is flying in Pittsburgh. The day has been a disaster and then the drive home was even worse. There were so many stupid drivers out there whenever it snowed. You would have thought they'd never driven in snow before. He's relishing the peace and quiet. That's when he thinks of her most. He's thinking now, that if he were in Palmetto he wouldn't have to worry about snow. "Damn it Tyler," he says. "Don't put yourself through this. You have to put this behind you once and for all."

At that precise moment the phone rings breaking his train of thought. He puts down his beer and bowl of popcorn to answer. "Hello."

"Hello, Tyler, how are you?" George asks on the other end of the line. "Got any of that white stuff flying around up there?" Of course he knows it's snowing there. He's just seen them show it on the weather channel. "Seems to me it could be a big one. It was in the low sixties here today and sunny."

"Did you call to harass me George? Tyler asks picking up his beer and taking a swig.

"No, not really, but I just caught it on the weather channel as I picked up the phone to call and I know you really love the snow, right?"

"Okay, if you didn't call to harass me, then why? And don't tell me you are checking up on me, because you just called me last week and nothing has changed."

"No, Tyler, I'm not checking up on you. I have some news," he says taking a deep breath. He'd dreaded making this call, but decided the sooner he gets it off his chest the better off he'd be. Tyler wouldn't be, but that isn't going to be his problem.

"What is it George? Are you going to retire?" Tyler asks jokingly.

"Don't I wish and aren't you being funny. Tyler, Sam's engaged and getting married Christmas Eve," he says knowing this will be a blow. "Damn!" Tyler says out loud.

"What?" George asks.

"Nothing, I just said damn. How long have you known George?"

"Just found out today. Sam told me this morning. Tyler, this is bittersweet news for me, but I know it's gonna be hard for you. Hey man, I know you still love her. Why else would you be calling and checking in on her so much? I wasn't going to tell you because I know you might try to win her back, now that you know she's getting married. I'd hate like hell for you to cause a stink, but I also know you have to do what's best for you. You do with the information what you want, but God help you Tyler, if you hurt her. Think real hard before you make a move. Do you hear me?"

There is silence on the other end and George doesn't know if Tyler's hung up. "Tyler you still there?"

"Yes, I'm still here. George, I love her so much," he says feeling the emptiness in his stomach again. It feels just like it did the day she walked out of his hospital room.

"I know you do Tyler, but think about it. You are the one that sent her away and you know what hell she went through and I lived it. You have to think now, if maybe in loving her you should let her go. If you come back now you might be rejected. Could you live with that? I'm not telling you that because I've talked to her, I'm just looking at it from all angles. I know it's taken her a long time to get over you. Is she still in love with you? I don't have the answer. But do you want to risk it?"

"Jesus, George. I wish I'd never picked up this receiver."

"Sorry man, but I knew you'd want to know. You know I'm here anytime you want to talk. If you decide to come to Palmetto will you let me know?"

"Sure. I've got some major thinking to do George. Thanks for calling." Tyler says taking the last sip of his beer. Looking at the can, he mentally notes he needs another one. "I'll talk to you soon."

"Don't be too hard on yourself Tyler. You only did what you thought was best for Sam. But you forgot to think about what was best for you and that you would have to live with the consequences."

"Don't remind me. I think about it everyday. Take care George and I'll talk to you soon," he says and hangs up.

Walking to the refrigerator he looks at the calendar on the pantry door and notes that Christmas Eve is only two weeks away. "Okay buddy," he says looking at the beer he's just retrieved from the fridge. "What the hell am I going to do now?"

Chapter Thirty-Three

Samantha feels she's in a whirlwind. It's only one week before the wedding. She's taken the week off from work. Of course George said it was okay. It helps when your boss feels he's your second father. Anything she wants she gets. He was pleased when she told him she and Todd were engaged, but she also knows he has a soft spot in his heart for Tyler. But being the man he is, he'd never ask her any questions. He'd just let her follow her heart too. And he has absolutely nothing against Todd. He just wants her to be happy.

All of the plans for the wedding are in order. The girls at the office had a shower for her, as did a couple of her aunts. Her house is covered with shower and wedding gifts. Todd has enjoyed the gifts just as much as she, but he particularly likes the unmentionables from the personal shower the girls at the office gave her.

She's going for her final fitting for her wedding dress today. The bridesmaid's gifts are ready and she needs to pick them up, then she's meeting Todd for lunch. He has a meeting, but thinks he can meet her by one o'clock.

Dressed in only her short red terry cloth wrap, which she's about to take off and step into the shower, she hears her doorbell ring. "Who can that be?" She wonders. She isn't expecting anyone. Not thinking of how she is dressed she goes and answers the door. She isn't ready for who is standing on the other side.

"*Oh my God!*" She exclaims.

"Hello, Sam," Tyler says blushing from the sight of her in that red terry cloth wrap. He'd always loved her in red. "Congratulations. I hear you're getting married."

"Tyler, what are you doing here?" She asks and at the same time looking down and realizing what she has on. Or better yet, what she doesn't have on.

"Sam, I'd like to talk to you if I may. I know I have no right showing up like this, but I know I can't live with myself if I don't."

Knowing it is probably the wrong thing to do she asks him in. "Please excuse me a minute won't you?" She blushes as she heads towards her bedroom to retrieve her robe. Glancing at the clock as she goes back to the living room, she knows she doesn't have much time. She's due for her fitting at ten.

"Tyler, I have a fitting at ten so you have to make this short." She says sitting down on the couch. "Have a seat, won't you?"

"Thanks," he says as he sits down in the chair that faces out the window looking at the ocean.

Looking out at the ocean and being in her cottage, is bringing back too many memories. "Sam, I'm not going to beat around the bush here. I want you to know I still love you and wanted to come here to see if I could have a second chance and make you change your mind about marrying Todd. I know I have no right in asking you this, but I couldn't live with myself if I don't at least try."

"*Boy you have a lot of nerve!*" She exclaims and notices she's starting to shake. "Do you know how many times I called your parent's house only be told you wouldn't talk to me and the number of times I left messages on your answering machine? If you love me like you say you do, why didn't you tell me that then?"

"I thought at the time I was doing the right thing. When I left the hospital I had no idea what kind of permanent injuries I was going have and I didn't want you stuck with an invalid, Sam," he explains.

"I loved you, Tyler, and I wanted to be with you to take care of you. I didn't care about the extent of your injuries. Didn't you realize that it didn't matter?" She asks and she knows she isn't going to be able to hold the tears back much longer.

"All I saw was this beautiful, young and vibrant young lady that I didn't want to see spending the rest of her life with me. I'd already felt guilty enough about taking you off to the university and getting you hurt. Then if it had ended up that I would have had permanent injuries also, that would have been too much to put you through. I couldn't do that to you, Sam. That is how much I did love you and still do. I was willing to give you up so you could find happiness."

"*Damn you, Tyler!*"

She shouts and the tears are now streaming down her cheeks. "Couldn't I have made those decisions myself? I wasn't a little girl anymore. I knew what I was doing and what I wanted!"

"At the time Sam, I thought it was the only answer. The day you walked out of that hospital was the worst day of my life. I haven't stopped thinking about you for a minute." He says getting out of his chair and kneeling down in front of her. "Sam, I love you, you know that. Can you give me another chance, or am I too late?"

Crying uncontrollably now she's having a hard time speaking. "This isn't fair Tyler. I'm getting married this Saturday. And what about Todd? He's been my life support. He saw me through this whole mess. If he'd walk in here right now it's hard telling what he'd do to you. Do you know that?"

"I'm sure it wouldn't be pretty. But right now I would take my chances," he says wiping the tears from her face with the back of his hand.

But I'm sure he won't want to be married to you if he knows you still love me."

And he knows he's really going out on a limb saying it.

"Tyler, I'm sorry," she says not knowing exactly why she uses the word sorry. She doesn't have any reason to be sorry. "Seeing you at that door brings back all those memories. I loved you so much and the times we had together I will never forget. And, yes, to answer your question, I do still love you and always will. But I've learned to live without you and I'm in love with Todd now and I *am* going to marry him on Saturday. I can't go back and I think you know that. I've gotten my second chance for love now with Todd. And I'm not going to risk losing it again.

Tears are now streaming down Tyler's face also. Samantha isn't so inconsiderate that she doesn't feel sorry for him, and finds herself wiping away his tears. At that moment he pulls her up off the couch and puts his arms around her. "God, I love you, Sam, and I always will," he says realizing that he's lost her. And at that moment he kisses her for the last time. The kiss is strong and he knows deep in his heart that she really does love him, but that she isn't going to forgive him.

"Tyler, don't," she says pushing herself away from him.

She can't be in those arms any longer, it's too dangerous.

"Thanks for letting me be here at all, Sam."

"Tyler, you need to go. I have to make this appointment."

"I'll go, Sam. Please be happy and for God's sake if you ever need anything you know where I am," he says walking to the front door.

"Thanks Tyler. I know I'll be happy, but I won't need you for anything, I'll have Todd."

"Good bye, Sam. I'll never forget you and what we had," he says as he kisses her on the cheek, gives her one last hug and opens the door. "Todd is a very lucky man, Sam."

Holding on to the door for support as Tyler walks out, she says. "I'll never forget you either Tyler. We *did* have something very special."

With tears streaming down his face he smiles back at her as he turns to walk away. He knows now that the time he spent protecting her wasn't the way she wanted to be protected. And now it is too late. He can't know what she's thinking behind the door she has just closed.

Getting into his car he shuts the door and all life just drains out of him. Slumping over the wheel he's never felt so alone. Not knowing exactly how long he sat there, he turns the key and starts the car. He's already made reservations at the local Inn, just in case. Just in case was all for nothing now.

Samantha watches Tyler as he walks down the driveway towards his car. Knowing how much she loves him made this moment even harder. She's sending the man she loves away. Has she completely lost her mind? Closing the door at that moment makes it seem final and she's beginning to wonder if she'd made a mistake. "If he just wouldn't have come here, I think I could have made it," she says to herself as she leans against the door and slides down to the floor completely drained. Seeing him brought back all of the terrific and also the tragic memories. The days they spent together she will never forget.

"Damn," she exclaims as she comes back to her senses. "I'm going to be late for my fitting." Getting up she wipes the tears off her face with her sleeve and heads for the shower.

Chapter Thirty-Four

Tyler somehow arrives at the *Carolina Tribune*. He wants to see George before he heads back to Pittsburgh. It will be his last trip to Palmetto. As long as Sam is here, he won't be able to ever come back. The memories will hurt too much. But he owes George at least this much. He's been such a good friend.

George is in his office with his nose to the grindstone when Tyler arrives. He taps on the door frame because George has left his office door open. "May I come in?" Tyler inquires.

"Tyler!" George exclaims surprised to see him. "What are you doing here?" And he doesn't need to ask anymore. He can see it in his eyes. "Don't tell me you've been to see Samantha. Have a seat man, you look like *you* just lost your best friend," he says coming around his desk as Tyler walks in.

"I did," he says. "I went to see her, George. Maybe it was the wrong thing to do to her but I had to try. When she answered the door she obviously wasn't expecting anyone. She was only wearing that red terry wrap because she was headed for the shower when I knocked. My God, just seeing her again in that, was too much."

George went to his private cabinet and was pouring Tyler a much-needed drink. "Here drink this, it might not help, but it can't do any harm either."

"Thanks, George," was all Tyler could say.

"You must have really shocked Samantha. How'd she take it and what did she say?" Obviously by the looks of you, it wasn't what you wanted to hear. Remember I cautioned you Tyler," he says and went to sit back down at his desk.

Tyler inhales the drink and tips the glass to George saying. "Thanks, I needed this. I know she loves me George, she told me, but she says she can't forgive me.

And that is what hurts most. She's gone and I'll never get to see her again," he says as the tears start again. "I just want happiness for her, George, really and I can't blame her for telling me no. God only knows I made the biggest mistake of my life."

"So what will you do now? Do you think you'll stay for the wedding or will you head right back to Pittsburgh?"

"No. I won't be going to the wedding. I didn't get an invitation and I doubt very much whether Todd would appreciate me being there anyway, nor Sam either for that matter. I've got a room at the Inn and I think I'll stay tonight and go back in the morning. I do love it here and it sure beats the hell out of winter up North.

"I'm sorry Tyler for everything. If it wasn't for me bringing you down here for that case, none of this would have happened. I managed to get both of you hurt physically and now your heart is broken also. I really made a mess of things."

"George none of that was your fault. You did the right thing in bringing me here. It was my idea to go to the university, not yours. And it was also my fault I fell in love with Sam. That's life George. I don't blame you for a thing. If anyone is to blame it is I."

Tyler's getting up to leave and George is lost for words for him, but manages to say. "Tyler I truly am sorry. If you'd ever want to come work for me, I'd be honored. You are welcome anytime."

"Thanks, but I don't think it would do me any good to see her here everyday. But I appreciate the offer.

"You bet." George says as he pats him on the shoulder. "Keep in touch will you?"

"Sure George, I will and you take care." He says as he walks out of George's office. Standing in the hallway he looks towards Sam's office one more time, then turns and walks out.

Chapter Thirty-Five

Samantha barely makes it to her fitting on time. She doesn't look the way she wants to for her final fitting, but it's all the energy she can muster up to even make it after Tyler left.

Looking at her watch she knows she's running close, to meet Todd. She just needs to stop at the jeweler's and pick up the gifts for the bridesmaids. She'd picked out white gold bracelets adorned with a yellow gold palmetto tree on top and is having them engraved on the inside with Todd and her names and their wedding date. The reason she's picked this particular bracelet is it signified the place on the beach where she fell in love with Todd. He'd previously purchased the necklace for her and at the time, she noticed there was a matching bracelet. The jeweler has them all wrapped and ready to go when she arrives, which saves her a few minutes.

Todd's waiting for her at the restaurant when she arrives. The hostess is taking her back to their table and as they approach she notices Todd looking at his watch. No doubt he's wondering how late she's going to be. He knew she was having her final fitting, but he thought he'd allowed her ample time for it.

Looking up from his watch he sees Samantha coming towards him, but she isn't yet close enough for him to see her face. "Took you a little longer than you expected?" He asks as the hostess pulls her chair out for her to be seated.

"Miss, may I get you something from the bar?" The hostess asks.

"Yes, please. I'll have a white Zinfandel," She says pulling the chair out next to her and placing the bag containing the bracelets and her purse on it. She's taking her time because she knows Todd will soon notice her discomfort, if he hasn't already seen it in her eyes.

"Samantha, are you alright?" He asks when he senses something is wrong. She looks like she's been up all night.

"I didn't have a very good morning Todd," she says just as the waiter comes to take their order. She hasn't had time to open the menu, let alone had time to even think about how she's going to tell him that Tyler's shown up.

Seeing that Samantha isn't ready to order, he motions for the waiter with his hand. "Sir can you give us a little time? I don't believe we are ready to order just yet."

"Sure, take your time. Just let me know when you are ready," he says and makes his way to another table of customers. The lunch crowd has thinned out so there is no hurry.

"Were there complications with your fitting, Samantha?" He asks needing to know what has gotten her so upset and made her late.

"No, the dress fits perfectly. In fact I'm going to pick it up tomorrow. They just want to press it before I take it home.

"Then what has you so upset?" He asks noticing that she is even shaking when she picks up the glass of wine the waiter brought.

Deciding the best way is to just say it she says. "Tyler came to see me this morning."

"*Tyler!*" Todd exclaims and looks around when he notices it comes out a little bit too loud. "What the hell does he want and what business does he have coming around a week before our wedding?"

She knows he's very sensitive when it came to discussing Tyler. He's been through too much with her and seen what he'd done to her. "Please let me explain," she says taking another sip of her wine.

"I'm sorry, Samantha. I didn't mean to react like that, but you know what I think of that guy." And he reaches across the table and takes her hand. "You are shaking so much. He must have really had an effect on you. Please tell me what he wanted."

Even though she knows that he isn't going to really want to hear it, she knows she's going to have to tell him. "He said he still loves me. He also said that the only reason he sent me away was because of his love for me. He didn't want me to have to take care of him the rest of my life if he'd been permanently affected by the accident. He wanted me to go on with my life."

"And what did you tell him, Samantha?" He asks not knowing if he actually wants to hear the answer and wondering just what did take place at her house this morning.

"Todd, I've never hidden the fact that I love him and always will. But I also told you my love has changed. I may love him, but I'm not in love with him. How could I be? From the first time we were together you took care of me. It wasn't about you and your needs, it was about helping me to get over Tyler. You gave me a shoulder to cry on, strength when I thought I couldn't go on without him, and courage to face each day and most of all love, when I thought I would never be able to love again."

Todd was speechless at what she is saying. The waiter had come and gone when he saw that they were deep in conversation and he'd picked up on what she was saying. He thought it was so touching, he quietly disappeared until later.

"But you haven't told me what you told Tyler."

"I don't think at this point it matters Todd," she says softly. "What matters is I told him I was marrying you and told him goodbye. He said you were the luckiest guy on this earth and he wishes us happiness."

Changing his tune he says. "That couldn't have been easy for him nor you, Samantha. I think I actually feel sorry for the guy.

He found out too late what he'd given up and I'm thankful to him for that."

"After all he put me through, I agree with you. I feel a little sorry for him too."

Tyler spends the rest of the day and night in the motel room. He has no desire to go out because he knows too many things here will remind him of Sam. The next morning after checking out he drives to the beach. He has to return one last time where he met her. The warm air is now cool and the beach is all but deserted. It's just like his relationship with Sam had been, so warm, now cold, and full of life and now empty. He walks back to his car and drives back to Pittsburgh.

Chapter Thirty-Six

The sun is going down and there is a little breeze. The temperature is higher than normal for being Christmas Eve. The church Samantha's attended since she was born is small, but she and her mother have decorated it beautifully. Samantha wanted it to be elegant and not the traditional red even though it is her favorite color.

There are fresh garlands hung around the stained glass windows with sprays of white poinsettias, roses and white velvet ribbons, around the arched top. Behind the altar is a continuous garland with the white swags strategically placed to hold it up.

A gold candelabra with white candles adorn the organ and there are one on each one of the window sills. Each of the pew bows are made the same as the sprays, except they used white tulle to enhance the back of the them so they stand out from the side. Two beautiful bouquets of white roses are on either side of the alter with gold candelabras behind each bouquet. The church is ready for an angel to walk down the isle.

Samantha can not believe it when she and her father are standing at the back of the church ready to descend the isle. It is absolutely beautiful. The candles are allowing only enough light to illuminate the white runner for her to see to walk down the isle. The sound of the organ playing the bridal march gives her goose bumps. And most of all, seeing Todd waiting at the end of the isle makes her the happiest girl in the world.

"Ready dad?" She whispers to him, putting her arm under his.

"Ready as I'll ever be. You look absolutely radiant!"

"Thank you. I love him with all my heart."

"I know you do," he says squeezing her arm as he leads her down to Todd.

Tyler's been standing at the back of the church the whole time. He came back for the wedding. What he's just witnessed breaks his heart, but he knows at the last minute he is doing the right thing. He'd actually come to stop the wedding, but seeing Sam look into Todd's eyes the same way she had his, he knows he has to let her go. He quietly exits the church before she has a chance to catch a glimpse of him standing there, when they come back up the isle. There would be no second chances for him